Dear Dan,

With Lasting

Admiration

from your friend

Love Jane.

x   x   x

June Yeo

2016.

Octopus Pirate

Table of Contents

Dedication of Octopus Pirate

Dedicated to my friend and mentor
Dan Thompson

Copyright:

Chapter 1

(Arm One).

The birth of the Octopus Pirate

Catherine gasped, she was feeling uncomfortably hot. She took out a clean white handkerchief and wiped the sweat beads from her forehead. Being on board a cruise ship had been the last thing she had wanted. Horace, her husband, had been newly appointed as captain. It was a big deal and he had expected her to accompany him and be a dutiful Victorian wife.

All around her jubilant people, dressed in their finest clothes, were gaily promenading around the deck of the ship. A string quartet played, Catherine recognised the song; it was Beethoven. The sweet notes, jollity lifting the air, would have made her smile normally, but not today as, although this was a large ship, in Catherine's heavily pregnant state the movements of the waves, however small, were violent enough to make her feel sick. She looked around at the faces of the passengers; she knew no one, nor did she want to. Their laughter sounded false and forced to her. She watched them, revolted, as they greedily drank the free champagne.

She looked down at her large belly, feeling overwhelmingly sad. She had not liked the thought of giving birth at sea, even although there was a good doctor and mini hospital on board. She hadn't imagined motherhood to be like this.

She thought of her home, a lovely red brick house, the open fireplaces and the beautifully decorated nursery ready for this much-anticipated first child. She had lovingly selected each new toy, the clockwork duck mobile, the musical tin top that had been handed down and cleaned up. She had scoured marketplaces and picked out teddy bears with red glass eyes and the softest velvet pink noses. She had sanded down and re-varnished an old bleached pine chest of drawers that now stood in the corner of the nursery, full of hand knitted jumpers from local old ladies, in lemon yellow wool with small wooden buttons.

Catherine let out a sigh. All right, she had known what being married to a sailor would be like, sailors were in her blood; they ran dark and red through her family history. Horace had also come from a long line of sailors. However, his ancestors had not set sail on such a fancy ship as this, as far back there was a rumour that they were pirates.

'The Empress,' was an impressive steamship. Catherine leant back on the top deck wall and admired the small gay bunting that fluttered in the wind. The smell from the buffet was rich and sweet and she felt salty bile build in her mouth. She turned and walked away from everybody; she did not feel like being sociable, she did not want to be there and the smell of the sticky food was making her feel more unwell.

Catherine walked past a glass viewing window showing the engine room and marvelled at the large steam pistons that pounded up and down, driving the large ship forward. The intricate clockwork dials spin at incredible speeds before her eyes. She peered down through the panel to the belly of the engine room where she could see men shovelling loads of coal into a large furnace. A copper boiler full of water hissed and bubbled above it, making the steam. From her vantage point, she was able to eye the cylinder and piston, which resembled a large bicycle pump piping the steam into the cylinder, causing the piston to move back and forth. The shine from the gleaming brass pistons was strangely hypnotic; the machine moved in a perfect sequence. The heat and the smell of the coal burning were overwhelming so Catherine walked on.

She reached the bow of the ship and was pleased to find she was alone. She walked to the railings and gulped deep breaths of the fresh cold salt air. Suddenly she began to feel a little faint, she swung around to call out for help, but lost her balance and plummeted deep into the icy waves.

The fear hit her at once; she would drown; she felt as if she was being pulled down deeper and deeper. The noise of the propellers was deafening.

Catherine looked up to the now far away surface; she could see the waves break above her. Her clothes were heavy; she did her best to climb out of them and desperately fought to get back up.

As she hit the surface, gasping for air, she saw the ship was now a good way in front, the waves from its large engines producing a surge in current that rocked Catherine.

Desperately treading water, she cried 'help!' But it was useless.

A sudden realisation reached her; no one knew she had fallen off the ship. No one was missing her. She had done her best not to socialise with the others; she had been aloof and not interested, almost sulking, as she was unhappy that she was expected to be there.

She paddled harder and harder in the water, waving her arms desperately. She had heard that there were sharks in this area, blood thirsty sharks; she knew that thrashing around like this was not a good idea, she would attract them.

She thought again about her house, the nursery, the new cot with yellow sheets and happy wallpaper, she thought briefly of her husband and longed for the safety of her mother's arms.

She watched the ship steam away. She knew it was hopeless; the sea was huge, vast, if they turned and came back to look for her, it would be like trying to find a needle in a haystack. She was not sure how long it would be before she was missed. Her husband, as captain, was busy, there was to be a grand dinner that evening. Being a perfectionist, he had taken it upon himself to arrange and oversee every small detail from the flowers to food to the music; he would be rushed off his feet.

An unkind glimmer of hope struck her; at the meal, she would be missed. She wistfully imagined the large dining hall with thousands of candles, the fine white porcelain plates, the delicate exotic food and the fragrant wine.

Catherine's heart sank; her legs and arms were getting tired. She tried to think what the time was. 'It must be around three in the afternoon and dinner was seven sharp.' Quickly she did the sum in her head. 'Four hours.' She was sure that she would be unable to paddle for four hours, even if she was not in her heavily pregnant condition.

Suddenly she felt sad for her unborn child; it overwhelmed her and she began to cry. 'The baby, the poor baby.' It had been so longed for and planned for. She felt a sudden pain; this was her first time as a mother, but she knew intuitively that was a contraction and knew that the baby was going to be born. Trying to calm herself, trying to dull the pain, she desperately looked out across the horizon. Nothing, the steamship was long gone; it had faded into the distance like a dream. Then a sudden calmness hit her, like an acceptance of her death, she stopped paddling and began to sink deeper and deeper, water starting to fill her lungs.

Then she felt the pain again from her womb, the baby was coming and it wanted to live.

Again she fought to the surface, using all her strength. She told herself that there must be something, some hope; she did not want to die like this. Again pictures flooded her mind, the ship, the happy party, the many strange laughing faces and she felt sickened by it. She hesitated as she saw them in her mind as if they turned and faced her, laughing at her in high pitched shrill bursts, their smooth faces smothered in heavy makeup. Their breath was stinking with alcohol, she could even smell it; it hung like a vomit perfume around her.

She cried out, almost screaming, 'help me! Please!' She started to pray, although she did not believe in God. She briefly thought about her childhood and how she had been made to attend church. Begrudgingly, she had attended; she had not wanted to give up her Sundays when she longed to be out in the wild countryside, climbing trees and playing with the leaves, running free like an eager deer, not dressed up in stiff clothes listening to lectures on the morality of life.

A thought struck her, a whisper, alone in the deep ocean; maybe this was a punishment from God, a punishment for not believing, for not listening, for pretending.

At that point, Catherine wanted to believe there was a God and that he would save her and if not her, at least, her unborn child. She paddled faster, hoping that this was true.

She chastised herself, why had she not made friends with the people on the ship, oh, why had she been so stubborn? Horace had wanted her to socialise; he had even implied that it was her duty to support him and to be a good wife.

A pang flared inside her again; the contractions were getting closer together, the pain almost unbearable. She lurched on her side in the water, the agony apparent only to herself. Catherine started to worry that any blood from the birth would attract sharks. She hurriedly scanned the water, staring around her, but there was nothing, not even the deafening sound of seagulls that she had become accustomed to hearing. Nothing, just the now peaceful waves lapping upon each other and the hovering of the larger waves in the distance. Then ahead she saw a large clump of seaweed. Desperately, she made her way over to it with a struggle, then hung on to its side limply to catch her breath. Slowly and with much effort, she pulled herself onto it and began forcing herself as near to the centre as she could.

The weed mat was a condensed mass of seaweed, an uneven natural life raft. After she had climbed onto it, she found herself to be still submerged two inches in the sea water as her weight took the seaweed mass below the surface; however, she was grateful she was able to rest at last. The pains were getting closer and closer together. Catherine tried to distract herself by staring at the teeming life that appeared to live around the natural floating island. There were also sorts of brightly coloured small fish that darted around her and larger comical looking crustaceans.

Just as she was starting to relax, the baby pushed again. Catherine shouted, 'Help me!' more in frustration than in pain.

She began to question herself, why was she here? Why oh why did she go off on her own and stand so close to the rail? Was it her way of tempting fate? She had no one to blame but herself, but in spite of this and to help to keep hold of her sanity, Catherine started to blame her husband. Why, she thought, why could she have not stayed at home? Why was he so selfish as to make her come on this trip?

Once more, she thought of her own room, her comfy bed, her flowery wallpaper and the blue chintz curtains.

A sharp pain again formed in her belly. Gasping for air, she became drained of energy. That was the largest contraction so far. She screamed with agony, knowing that she had to push. This baby was going to be born whether or not she wanted it to be so; it made no difference.

Her thoughts turned towards the hope of rescue, could there be a chance they would be found alive? She had to hope so, she wanted to believe that ship would turn back to find her, but, in reality, she was not sure how far she had drifted already. Her mouth was dry, she longed for a drink and, as if the gods had taken mercy on her, the clouds suddenly burst, sending warm rain down onto her fragile body. She scooped this gratefully into her hands and drank. The water made her feel calmer and, with one last push, the baby was born.

She had nothing to cut the cord with, and nothing to wrap the now screaming child in. She pushed the baby to her breast and watched motionlessly as it took its first sustenance from her.

On board the ship, Horace checked his pocket watch. It was seven o'clock. He was dressed in his full uniform. He had been busy all day so had not missed Catherine, but now he glanced over at the seat next to himself; his wife's empty chair.

A silent, angry thought hit him, why is she late? She knows this is important to me. Horace screwed up his eyes and scowled at the door, expecting her hurried entrance, her flustered face and the late apology. He turned his attention to a glass of red wine in front of him, lifting it up; first admiring the redness of the colour, then brought it forward to his nose and breathed in its delicate, full bouquet before tempting himself with a sip. He raised his glass to a wealthy couple sat across from him. The overdressed pair, two plump ladies who were snugged tightly into their whalebone corsets, giggled as they raised their half empty glasses back.

Horace, impatient, signalled to one of the waiters. 'Go and find my wife and bring her to me.'

The waiter left the room and walked along the windswept deck towards the Captain's quarters. Not finding her there, he gathered some crew members to help search the ship.

Ten minutes later, when no one had arrived, the captain threw down his serviette in temper and walked out of the dining hall to get her himself.

He was met by whispering in the hallways.

'Where is my wife?' Horace demanded when he saw the waiter.

The waiter went white. 'We've looked everywhere,' he said nervously.

'Everywhere!' the captain shouted. 'She must be on board, I know this is a large ship, but Catherine must be somewhere.'

He paced across the deck before issuing his next order. 'Everyone, stop what you are doing and make it your priority to find Catherine! She must be found. She is heavily pregnant and could go into labour at any moment.' An urgent tone was reflected in his voice. Horace tried to think the last time he had seen Catherine and believed it to have been the first thing that morning when they had breakfasted together.

He was angry with himself; he had been too busy with the preparations for the party. This was his first time on board the ship as captain and he had felt duty-bound to oversee every detail; it had been of paramount importance to him.

Of course, he had noticed that his wife had not been around that day, but had put that down to her being pregnant. She needed rest and quiet; he knew that.

Everybody searched the ship but found nothing. The captain, visibly shocked, knew that could only mean one thing. She had fallen overboard. It was getting dark; the lights were on already switched on throughout 'The Empress.' The small strings of red, green and yellow lights swayed in the sea breeze which played around the decking.

'We must stop the ship and turn back!' Horace ordered. The cry went out the engine halted, the course re-plotted.

'You and you,' the captain said, pointing to two of his crew. 'Get spot lamps on the bow of the ship. All spare hands, look out!'

Meanwhile, in the dining room, the grand party went on, not knowing of the mayhem unravelling around them.

The captain rushed up to the helm and ordered a signal to be sent out to all ships in the area on the route they had travelled.

He was going to turn the ship back. In his heart, he knew it was futile, but he had to try.

He waited impatiently as the Morse-code signal was tapped out, desperate for any news to come back. But nothing came, just endless silence.

After two hours he returned to the deck and watched as the spotlights bounced hopelessly over the water's surface, only flashing back and illuminating black patches of the cold sea.

It was midnight, the noise from the party in the dining room had hit fever pitch. Everyone was drunk and laughing loudly; all were unaware of the tragedy playing out or even the change in the ship's course.

The captain was weary, he had had a long day arranging frivolity, he was very angry with himself now for putting such importance on such trivial things. The tiredness shaved his eyes which burned with fatigue, but he could not bring himself to pull them away from the beams of light that skipped off the water in front of him.

He thought about his wife with tenderness. He had fallen in love with her in one moment, the very first time he had seen her. Her father was also a seaman and Horace had called around to deliver a message from the shipping company. Catherine was in the house and had brought tea things into the room. Her strong, wiry black hair shone against her soft pale skin. She had deep brown large eyes that he had inextricably fallen into.

She poured the tea and Horace could not stop looking at her. He was captivated. Catharine handed him a cup, her soft perfume warming him and filling his heart. Their hands briefly touched and he felt an electric tingle shoot up his arm and bring a red flush his face. He was in love, smitten, from then on.

Catherine, in her early twenties, was a striking natural beauty. From a small child, she had known that she wanted to be an artist and illustrate books. She had her whole life planned out; she had already attained her qualifications and was arranging to finish her art studies in Paris. This chance meeting over a cup of tea with Horace had pushed her life into another direction completely.

Horace made his intentions plain there and then; he was not a man to beat around the bush. He was sure that his proposal would be accepted; he was proud and determined. He always knew what he wanted the second he saw it and made an immediate effort to get whatever it was. Luckily for Horace, Catherine's father admired him and thought him to be more than a suitable match for his daughter. Within a few weeks, they were married and settled into their new home, Cherry Tree Cottage, as picturesque as it sounded.

Now contently married and a homemaker, Catherine plunged with earnest into the small house's decoration, painting murals on the walls, creating magical planting arrangements in the wind blown garden. She enjoyed the simple pleasures that homemaking brought, such as arranging posies of fresh flowers each day in the living room and hallway to welcome any callers. She also had kindled a new love of baking and enjoyed making fresh bread and jams and inventing her own cake recipes.

As Horace thought about their home at that point, it seemed so very far away and he could not imagine living there without Catherine. She loved Cherry Tree Cottage and he had worked alongside her to get the nursery ready for their child. An icy wind blew up from the sea and Horace's heart was struck dead. He braced himself as the hero he was, feeling punch-drunk as a tear sniffed its way down his cheek and the realisation that the love of his life would never see home again.

He was lost in his own morbid thoughts. The next time he looked at his watch, it was six in the morning, the sun had tripped its way up over the horizon as the port they had set sail from only yesterday came back into view. He could see the sun rising, colouring the small houses dotted along the cliff a dusky pink. Everything looked so beautiful that, for a fleeting moment, his heart skipped a beat. The seagulls coasted above the ship, screeching an ear-splitting cry which welcomed and signalled their early return.

Horace let out a deep sigh. Catherine was lost at sea. His child would never breathe life and he would never get to hold either of them. A grey shadow drifted across his face and remained with him.

And so it was in this story so far. Horace, although trying all search means at his disposal, came to give up within just one week.

But this is what happened. Days later, out at sea, in amongst the floating bed of weeds, Catherine had given up her struggle to live. The baby lay on her chest, crying with hunger. It was then, from the depth of the sea, an octopus arose. Its arms tenderly explored the baby lying upon the weeds, sensing the small life and the baby's plight. Without wasting further time, it sent the body of its dead mother to find her rest in a watery grave below. Then, wrapping an arm around the baby and gripping the weed mat in its beak, the octopus sucked the water into its body and propelled itself backwards at great speed to drag the seaweed mat toward hope. Which was found in an unexpected place.

Chapter 2

(Arm 2).

The Octopus Pirate's Childhood

Days later the small seaweed mat washed up on the shoreline of an old monastery nestled on an island off the mainland of Scotland. Mary, the only occupant, a strong devotee to God, being a former nun, lived there as a self-imposed recluse.

Mary spotted the baby as she bought in her fishing boat. When she saw it, she quickly tied her boat up and ran over to the weed mat, wading ankle-deep into the water to retrieve it. Mary examined the baby, noticing strange tube-like growths on the back of its neck that looked a bit like an octopus' suckers. Undaunted, she gathered the baby up in her arms and carried him carefully the short distance up the twisty path towards her home.

Mary lived at the top of the cliff in a small, well-built house joined onto the back of an old church. Although Mary was no longer a nun, she held on to the beliefs and practices of the order, such as banning all frivolous wants. Her home and the church were usually kept unheated and at times were so cold that she could see her own breath. Mary, now aware of the weakened condition of the tiny life she carried, rushed to light the old boiler and turn the heating on.

The church and the house were served by a linked and antiquated under floor heating system which rattled and banged from the sudden shock of being brought back into life.

She wrapped the baby in a soft wool blanket and carefully placed him on the sofa. Then she set to work busying herself, warming goat's milk and arranging a make-shift bed out of an old cupboard drawer.

She began making clothes for the baby. She felt so happy that she sang and cooed to him. 'A baby, what a gift from God you are, little one.'

Mary fed the baby and cradled him until he fell asleep. She reflected on the change this child would bring. Mary's life had become almost routine for the last ten years or so since she had retired from being a nun and been gifted the island she now inhabited.

Since setting up home there, she had lived a solitary existence, only making infrequent visits to the nearby mainland when a church occasion had taken her fancy. Generally, on the whole, she saw no one, apart from one old friend, Anne, who was also a nun. Anne came to visit every fortnight and brought supplies which she traded for Mary's goat's cheese.

Mary looked forward to Anne's visits as she also brought not only news from the mainland but new stray cats for her to look after. Mary liked to rescue cats and by the time the baby arrived, she had amassed twenty, which she fed with the fish she caught by going out in her small fishing boat. Mary also used this time alone to meditate and pray. Her cats were used to her routine and would wait on the jetty for her. She lived on the island quite self-sufficiently and cheaply, mostly eating fish and the vegetables that she grew in her garden. A good planner, she pickled vegetables and kept them in underground stores alongside the fermenting goat's cheese. However, she still valued Anne's visits and news from the mainland.

It was a week later to the day that her old friend Anne came for a visit. She was in a good mood; as she tied her small boat to the jetty, she sang gospel songs at the top of her voice and thanked God inwardly for the wonderful weather and good crossing. She carried a small cloth bag containing balls of white wool for Mary to knit into a jumper and knew that she would be pleased with the gift.

Mary was out in the shed, milking her goats ready for the next planned batch of cheese when Anne arrived. Mary was hoping that Anne would be bringing some more goat food when she visited that day; she was also wondering what her friend would make of the baby.

After a lot of thought and making lists of possible biblical names, Mary had named the baby Coco, after her favourite character in the book Pinocchio.

Coco was a good baby and Mary had already become genuinely emotionally attached to the boy in the short time since she had found him.

Anne made her way up to the old stone church, looking about for her friend. She climbed the twisty cliff path, still joyfully singing as she went. The island looked particularly beautiful that morning with the sun resting on it. Along the edges of the path grew small wild white and pink flowers which she studied with pleasure to take her mind off the arduous climb. As Anne reached the church, she called out to her friend's name and pushed open the large wooden doors.

No answer. The first thing Anne noticed was that the church was warmer than normal. She held her hand over the grate on the floor to test the warmth and was puzzled to find that the heating was on. Anne walked through the church and into Mary's living quarters at the back, still calling out her name. She could smell a wonderful fragrance of warming soup coming from the kitchen, beef soup which smelt like it also contained celeriac and squash.

'Mary, Mary,' Anne called in a musical way as her heart was still full of joy from the pleasant trip. When no answer came, she put down her cloth bag and hung her thick wool coat over a chair. She went over to the stove top to first sniff and then stir the large pot of soup, then added a pinch of salt and saffron to it. The smell was, even more, heavenly now she was up close and her mouth watered. She longed to take a sip, but thought better of it and returned to the table to sit down and look about her. It was then she heard a faint cry. At first Anne thought it was one of the many cats meowing, so took no notice. But then the crying became much louder, so she decided to investigate.

Anne walked into the next room and went over to a blanket lined drawer placed on a low table next to the window. She thought she saw movement and caught her breath. She peered in and gazed down in disbelief at the crying infant. Instinctively she picked it up and cradled it. The baby stopped crying, and Anne gently examined the tubes at the back of its neck, while singing a lullaby to calm it.

Just the Mary came into the room, slammed down the pail of goat's milk and rushed over to try and take the baby out of Anne's arms.

'Mary?' Anne was alarmed by her friend's unwelcoming behaviour.

'I found him!' Mary snapped before Anne could even get the question out.

'Found a baby, but where?' Anne asked, handing the boy over to Mary and looking bewildered.

'I found him on a bed of seaweed, washed up on the shore about a week ago,' Mary said in a fraught tone. She placed the baby over her shoulder and started rubbing his back.

'But where did it come from? Where's its mother?' Anne hastily asked.

'I'm not sure there is a mother,' Mary snapped back. 'I think he was abandoned, poor lamb, cast out to sea, just like in the Bible story, Moses in the basket. I believe that God sent this baby to live with me.' Mary cradled the baby, smiling and cooing at him.

Anna was horrified and shouted at her friend. 'Think, Mary, that can't be right! Why would anyone abandon their child like that?'

Mary answered in a bitter voice, holding Coco tight to her body, 'Maybe because of the strange growths on the back of its neck, maybe they did not want a freak for a son, put him on a mat of seaweed, pushed it out to sea and let the current take it.'

Anne's voice softened. 'That's possible, I suppose. After all, there's been no mention of a missing baby on the mainland. I can take him to the orphanage when I go home later.'

'No!' shouted Mary. 'The baby wasn't wanted by its mother. God gave me the baby to look after; I'll do that. I named him Coco, and I'll teach him everything I know about fishing and island life. And when he's old enough he can choose himself to leave if he wishes.'

'Mary, have you lost your marbles? I mean, you're out here all alone, what if there's a problem and the child needs a doctor or something? Be reasonable,' Anne pleaded.

'I am being reasonable. I can school the boy, God will provide all our needs, and if the worst comes to the worst, I can row back to the mainland,' Mary retorted and then looked down at Coco. Her whole face began to beam with light.

Anne could see there was a bond between them, she also knew her friend, and once her mind was made up there was no way of changing it, so changing the subject, she asked. 'Is that soup I smell?'

'Yes it is, Anne, let's eat!' Mary said, placing Coco back into the makeshift cot and rushing over to get two large willow pattern bowls from the dresser for the soup.

So Coco's fate was decided: he stayed on the island and grew healthy and happy and the years passed, and Mary grew to love him dearly, and Coco returned Mary's love. They lived as happily as two peas in a pod on their small island home.

True to her word, Mary taught him everything there was to know about life on their island and the mainland, as well as lessons from the many books left behind by the monks who used the church as a small monastery. She taught Coco how to read and navigate from the stars and all types of basic science and maths. When Mary felt that Coco was old enough to understand, she told him how she had found him, washed up ashore and how she named him after a character in her favourite story.

Coco asked Mary about what she thought the tube-like things were on the back of his neck, but even although they searched all the old books they had they couldn't find an answer. Coco grew quickly and was a hard worker, a happy child who found joy in the smallest things. To Mary's delight, he was a natural fisherman and also enjoyed growing vegetables and milking the goats. Every evening Mary read to him from the Bible and his favourite stories. The stories that Coco liked the best were those about adventures at sea and gruesome pirates. Although Coco was a good reader, he loved to hear Mary's voice as there was something very calming and soothing about it. It was true Mary's voice had a magical essence to it, perhaps groomed from all the years of being a nun and of hard praying. All throughout Coco's childhood, Anne continued her bi-weekly visits, and Coco was always pleased to see her and to hear news.

One of Anne's duties on the mainland was to visit the prison and give counselling and guidance to the inmates.

Coco developed a dark interest and fascination with the prisoners on Death Row and the stories behind those who were hanged. Anne provided colourful descriptions of them. She loved to tell him all the gruesome details of the murderers and their deeds and delighted as she watched his face flash with shock. Mary did not approve of the tales and would tut loudly as the pair was enthralled by the news of the latest hanging.

It must have been Coco's ninth Christmas with Mary when she decided to take him on his first visit to the mainland. She wanted to go to a special religious ceremony, a missionary called William Brown, originally from Mary's convent, was coming to the mainland to give a talk at a service. Mary had heard many stories from Anne about William Brown's good deeds and admired him greatly, so she did not want to miss his visit. There was to be another guest speaker as well from London; someone Mary had heard speak many times before when she was a nun. She was particularly fond of him as a speaker as she had put it, 'no one put God in perspective like that man did.'

Coco did not want to go and listen to the sermons. He had not been to the mainland before, and he wanted to explore. Secretly he wanted Anne to take him to the prison so he could talk to the men on Death Row, but he knew Mary would never allow him to do that as she disapproved of Anne even talking to him about the prisoners.

It was a hot sunny day when they arrived on the mainland. Coco pointed towards the beach in the distance, and Mary was quite happy to let him wander off and explore. Mary headed to the church. She believed the mainland was a safe place and so felt comfortable with her decision to allow Coco to walk around and explore the place rather than have him fidget while sitting next to her through the long service and the accompanying theoretical debate afterwards.

Coco skipped along the jetty away from the boat with a big smile on his face, eager for his adventure to begin. After about ten minutes, he came off the coast path and wandered along the sea front, looking in all the shop windows and admiring the sticks of rock on display. Soon he reached the end of the shops and saw a vast expanse of sandy beach in front of him. At first, he started to gather the small brightly coloured shells and pebbles but then his interest fell on a small group of bigger boys in the distance, standing around something, shouting at it and poking it with sticks.

Coco ran over, keeping a little way back from the boys and sticking his neck out so he could peer at the poor thing they were torturing.

To his surprise, he saw it was a giant octopus. It was moving slowly, painfully dragging its huge body across the sand, trying to get back into the sea. It stopped and looked directly at Coco, its large eyes pleading with him to give it some relief from the tormenting boys.

Coco felt his heart ache. The boys were much bigger than him, and there were many, he was outnumbered. He wanted to turn away, but still he felt the pull of the octopus' eyes as they locked with his. He had to do something: somehow, at that moment, he felt inextricably connected with the animal. He felt the blood pulse and pump through his veins, somehow he knew he was stronger, and his arms felt as if they were made of rocks. In that second, he was super human. He strode over to the boys and, knocking them aside, lifted the giant octopus above his head and threw it into the water.

The boys were taken aback; they were in shock. None of them could quite believe what had just happened.

They whispered among themselves, pointing at Coco while they stood back from him.

Coco had a glazed expression while standing as tall as his nine-year-old body frame would allow him. Shaking all over, he looked up and glared at them. His thoughts were not of the boys or even of the octopus that he had rescued; they were of himself. He felt different; he felt something had changed inside him, and Coco realized that the change had happened when the octopus had touched his arm with its suckers as he had lifted it up. It was as if he could communicate with the octopus. He glanced at the sea as he heard it say 'thank you' inside his head. Coco felt its emotions, fear and gratitude, as it swam safely away.

As he looked, one of the boys let out a shrill cry and pointed at Coco's neck. 'Look at his neck, there's something strange on it, he's a freak!'

Coco felt the back of his neck; the tubes were stuck out in a fan arrangement; they were taut and firm. He could still feel his blood pumping hard around his small body; his arms were thick and muscly. All of his senses were heightened; it was as if he could taste the venom in the boy's words.

Coco didn't run even although his mind was screaming for him to do so. Instead, he turned to look out at the sea. The octopus was now submerged under the waves. Coco, at last, felt free to move. As he turned back, he glared again at the boys, rendering them temporarily motionless.

They finally ran off, and Coco looked once more out to the sea and started to feel his body return to normal. It was then that he felt a firm hand on his shoulder. He swung around, relieved to find it was only Anne.

'Come on, Coco; come with me to my lodgings until it's time for you and Mary to go home. I've some hot chocolate and second-hand pirate books you might like to keep and a great new story to tell you about a new inmate on Death Row.'

Coco smiled and followed Anne back over the beach. He didn't tell her about the beached octopus and the mean boys as he had decided he didn't like the mainland and vowed never to come again.

Four more years passed and Coco remained at home alone every time Mary felt the urge to visit her old church on the mainland.

One morning Coco was woken up with the sound of soft piano music coming from downstairs, it was beautiful, and Coco felt that he had to follow it. Mary was playing Beethoven; he recognised it as Moonlight Sonata, which he knew was one of her favourites.

Coco went downstairs quietly and stood in the doorway, watching Mary. To Coco it appeared magical that this old lady could conjure up music that seemed very alive as her dry stiff hands flitted over the keys, transforming into enchanting music. It quite took his breath away. It had a timeless beauty.

When she had finished playing, he clapped his hands and said, 'bravo, bravo.'

Mary looked up, a strange expression washing over her face. Her eyes looked misty as if she had been crying.

Coco, realized something was wrong and nervously asked, 'what's wrong, Mary?'

She smiled and said, 'Oh, nothing. There's just something in that piece of music that reminds me of, when I was a young girl growing up in the countryside, miles from anywhere. My father was a farmer and loved to listen to Beethoven. My mother and I used to sit with him with the radio on and do our knitting. My mother was good at it; she knitted all my toys as a child.'

Coco thought about his room; he had several old knitted toys which used to be on his bed but were now relegated to the cupboard. When he was small, he would play with them for hours. Could they have been knitted by Mary's mother, he wanted to ask, but he noticed that Mary seemed lost in a dream world.

She stood up from the piano and started to dance around the room as if she was at a ball and had a man leading her. She danced to invisible music. Coco guessed, by the way, she was moving fast that the song in her head must have an upbeat and happy melody.

'Where are you now?' he asked, grabbing her open hand and waltzing around the small room with her.

Mary giggled and said, 'Oh I'm just remembering when I was a teenager, a little older than you are now, Coco. There was a time once in the autumn; we had a big feast with pumpkins and fruit and all the harvest. The local church had a big feast and all the children from the village, gathered around, and we danced and ate and laughed. Autumn has always been my favourite time of year.'

Coco dropped Mary's hand and started at her intently. 'Why did you become a nun, Mary?' he asked.

'God chose me,' Mary said firmly. 'I believed in God then, and I still do. You know, Coco, when a woman becomes a nun, they say vows to God the same as marriage vows and look, we are given a ring.' Mary stretched out her hand in front of Coco so that he could see the ring.

'Oh,' said Coco. 'Did you never want to marry a human man and have children of your own?'

Mary shook her head. 'I knew from an early age that I was chosen to do God's work and to be his servant. To begin with I did long to have children, more so when I was young and saw babies, but the years passed, and the need did not feel so great. Then when I had quite forgotten about having children, you were washed on up the shore like a forgotten far away wish, a gift. I believe God sent you to me in my old age, so we could love and care for each other.'

Coco smiled at her, and she laughed and took his hand and continued to dance, and then Mary asked, 'Is it alright for you do to the goats this morning? I'm feeling a little melancholy and would like to play some more piano.'

'Yes of course,' Coco said and ran upstairs to get dressed and then out to milk and feed the goats.

When Coco came back into the church with the pail of goat's milk, he heard piano music trickle in from the back room. It was a lively song and Coco felt his feet slightly twitching as he walked in to watch Mary at the piano. He stood watching her for the longest time, and it must have been the third song when he heard Mary start to sing. Coco gave Mary a curious, happy look. He was surprised; he had not her sing for such a long time. She had a lovely voice, somewhere around a mid-soprano. It was warm and welcoming.

After the song, he walked over and hugged Mary and stayed with his arms around her shoulders. Mary laughed.

'That was great,' he said. 'It's been so long since I heard you sing; please sing another song.'

'No, no,' Mary said. 'I don't really like to sing. I used to have to sing all the time when I was a nun.'

Coco, puzzled, asked, 'were you happy as a nun?'

Mary stood up and looked at him. 'Oh yes, very happy, to serve God was what I wanted to do. I was a missionary for years, although I found that a bit more of a test of faith than a service. As I've told you, Coco, I believe in God, he is my friend, always there when I worry about things, always there when I need a friend. And when I leave this earth I know that he will be there waiting for me, and I will be an angel swimming in the sky.'

Mary stood up and spun around the room with her arms spread wide like she was already an angel flying among the stars.

'Do you really believe that?' Coco asked. Looking at her, he could not bring himself to follow Mary's ideal, no matter how many Bible stories she read to him, but at the same time thinking how wonderfully comforting it was for her to believe that she would be an angel one day.

Mary didn't answer; she danced around the room with a big smile on her face and a dreamy look in her eyes, lost in her own imaginary game. Then, as if something important had jolted into her mind, she stopped and told Coco, 'I must go and write things down in my journal, it's important to me as you will have this journal. I won't always be here for you. I'm very old now, I'm not even sure how long I've been living here alone, I gave up counting birthdays when I first came when I was in my 70s. I think only God knows how long ago that was.' She let out a small thin laugh.

Coco studied Mary's face and was concerned as it almost seemed as if she worried about death suddenly. He did not like to think of her dying; he could not tell how old she was. He had noticed that the joints in her fingers did not work as well as they used to when she milked the goats. But he put the thought out of his mind, and everything remained perfect on the small island for another two years.

Until one morning, fifteen years to the day when Coco had been washed ashore. Then it changed.

Mary started to develop dementia. Coco noticed something was wrong almost immediately and could pinpoint the day as it started with the smallest of happenings.

Mary had been in the kitchen making bread and Coco had run into chat with her that morning after milking the goats. Mary had her hands in the flour mixture, but seemed troubled and said, 'I'm sure I have forgotten something.' She looked about the kitchen in an uneasy and doubtful way.

Coco was instantly worried, but tried to make light of it and jokingly said, 'come on Mary; you never forget anything.'

Mary looked up from the bowl. She didn't smile but said, 'I know it sounds strange, Coco, but I've forgotten how to light the stove.'

Coco could not hide his worry. He placed his arm around her shoulder and handed her a towel to wipe her hands and said, 'you'd better rest, Mary, you've been overdoing it lately, and you're not as young as you used to be.' He smiled at her and said, 'I'll finish the bread for you and do the chores. Go and rest for a bit.'

Mary nodded and wiped her hands before going to lie on her bed.

Later, Coco went into her room with a cup of tea to find that Mary was just lying on her side, looking blankly at the ceiling.

Coco put the cup on the bedside table and stroked her forehead softly. Then after about ten minutes, Mary drifted into a deep sleep, and Coco covered her with a large blanket and went to finish all the chores before bedtime.

Before Coco went to bed that night, he tiptoed into Mary's room and sat watching her sleeping for a while. She seemed peaceful. Relieved, he went to his own room and fell asleep reading a book about a man marooned on an island where he made pets of the dragons.

He was woken some hours later by the loud banging of doors slamming in the distance. He sat up and listened and figured that the doors blowing were in the church. Coco pulled on his dressing gown, crossed the kitchen, ran through the church and hurried to close them. The weather was awful, heavy rain and squally winds. Coco fought with the wind to close the large doors. He shut one and then gripped the other in both hands. As he started to close it, he glanced down to the sea's edge and in panic let the open door fly from his hands. Coco could see that Mary was casting off one of the boats and making ready to take it out in the bad storm. Alarmed, he rushed down the path after her, screaming her name to stop. When he reached the small jetty, he hurriedly cast off the other boat and set off after Mary, sailing as fast as he could towards her.

The waves were so high he only caught glimpses of her as the boat was lifted up and down on the swells of the current.

Coco had never been out at sea in waves this fierce before, but all his thoughts were for Mary. What was she thinking? Mary was everything in his world, his only family. Coco felt a lump forming in his throat and a sick feeling in his stomach. He was terrified of losing her. As he got closer to Mary's boat, Coco called out her name again, shouting on the top of his voice over the storm, 'Mary, Mary!'

Mary did not appear to have heard or even to have seen Coco. Instead, she stared intensely and blankly into the water. She believed that she could see some of the characters from one of her favourite books under the water smiling at her, calling and beckoning to her to follow them. 'I'm coming, I'm coming,' Mary said in a trance-like state as she stared down into their imaginary faces.

Coco battled to get his boat nearer to Mary's, he panicked and shouted again as he could see her hovering on the side of the boat, looking down into the deep water, trembling with cold. Coco was shocked to see that Mary only had her nightgown on, and her skin was ice white.

'Mary, stop, please stop!' Coco shouted; his heart was beating so loud it masked the noise of the waves. The little boats rocked from side to side in a terrifying way as the sea was so fierce.

Coco was almost alongside Mary's boat when he heard a cry from her and feared a tragedy was about to happen.

The waves swelled up and began to lurch high alongside his boat. The sea was rough; Coco had to battle the waves. Finally, he got the little boat close enough and reached out to grab Mary's outstretched hand, only to clasp it and then lose the grip as her hand slipped through his fingers.

Coco gasped in horror as she jumped in. Mary appeared not to have seen Coco as she was transfixed by the characters under the waves and dived down to be with them.

'No!' screamed Coco in complete fear.

His boat washed back, and he skilfully steered it over to where she had jumped in and stared down into the depths. He could see Mary floating under the water. The wind picked up around him and the small sails billowed with the force, the ropes making a rickety noise as they slapped against the wood. Coco steadied himself on the side of his boat and was just about to dive in after her when the beam of the sail was caught up by the wind and forcibly swung back, crushing his arm, breaking it. The pain was horrendous, and Coco screamed in agony but managed to push the beam off his arm, which was left hanging limply against his body. He searched the water again; he could still see Mary's body floating near to the surface.

His boat pitched to and fro; Coco stood up and steadied himself again, holding his breath he jumped in and dived down. The waves washed him away from the spot, but again, he dived down towards Mary and, this time, managed to grab her with his good arm and battled back to the surface again, keeping her head above the water. He tried desperately to push her body back on board the nearest boat, but with a broken arm, it was impossible. He cried out in frustration, 'no!' the waves started to get worse and lap over his head. He could tell that Mary was breathing shallowly but could sense that life was slipping away from her.

Somehow he emitted a superhuman strength. With his head under the water, Coco breathed through the tubes at the back of his neck and then blew out of his mouth. He was able to propel himself backwards at great speed, dragging Mary with his good arm.

In no time at all he was back on land and collapsed on the shore. At first, he was too weak to move further. Worried, he looked at Mary, she was unconscious but still breathing, Coco had never seen her like this, and he suddenly realized how small she was and fragile looking. The realization unsettled him, and he stood up and pulled Mary up the beach as carefully as he could. Coco knew there was no way he could make it up the twisting path to the church. He started to gather bits of wood and make a makeshift cover for them both out of tarpaulin and cuddled Mary to share his body warmth.

Frightened and in shock, Coco is relieved that Mary is, at least, alive. The storm began to quieten down, and the rain stopped. Coco fell asleep next to Mary.

Early the next morning Anne came to the island. It wasn't her time for a visit normally, but she was worried about the storm, which had also ravaged much of the mainland in the night and she was concerned at the two of them being alone on the island.

First Anne went to the house and the church, but could only find the hungry cats. She fed the cats and went outside, calling Coco's and Mary's name as loud as she could.

Coco heard and shouted to her. 'Anne, Anne, come quickly, Mary's hurt!'

Anne ran over and was shocked to find them outside in their night clothes and Mary unconscious. Worried, she asked what happened.

Coco quickly explained. 'Mary's not herself; she's been acting strange, forgetting things and last night she headed out to the sea and dived under the water. I was about to jump in when the beam on my boat swung over and crushed my arm. I managed to swim back with her but now I think my arm is broken.' Coco began to feel much happier now that Anne was there.

Anne looked at his arm and then at Mary, not sure what to say at first, then said, 'we need to get her out of that wet nightgown and tuck her up in a warm bed.'

Coco agreed, and the two of them did their best to carry Mary up the path. Anne undressed Mary and dried her, put a clean nightgown on her and covered her over with the blankets and made her comfy. Coco put the kettle on so that Anne could fill a hot water bottle. As Anne slipped the hot water bottle, wrapped in a towel, into Mary's bed, she noticed Mary didn't open her eyes but mumbled under her breath.

'What's that, Mary?' Anne enquired, holding her ear as near as she could, but not being able to understand any of the words. Anne held Mary's hand and said, 'there, there, rest now, everything will be ok now, you're safe at home in bed, and Coco is safe too, rest now.'

When she had finished saying the words, she looked at Mary's face, and a peacefulness appeared to sweep over her.

Anne left the room, leaving the door slightly ajar.

Coco was so exhausted he could hardly stand. He had got out of his wet clothes and gone back to the kitchen with a large blue blanket wrapped around him. He began to shiver more from the shock of the events rather than the cold. Anne came in and smiled at Coco reassuringly, then walked over to him so to properly examine his arm.

'Yes, that looks as if it's broken,' she said.

She went to get the first-aid box and bound and dressed Coco's arm.

Coco poured the tea with his good arm, and while sipping, Anne said, 'I think you should both leave the island.' There was a long pause and then she continued, 'after my tea I'll row back to the mainland, make the preparations and arrange for someone to collect you.'

Coco looked angry and said, 'look, Mary seems out of it at the moment. I'm not sure moving her would a good thing, the sea's still quite rough. I think she needs to rest. I can look after her.'

Anne said in a softer tone, 'Coco, I know you care for her, but I think Mary needs a doctor.'

Coco looked thoughtful. 'Then one should come and see her. I'm sure you can arrange it.'

Anne nodded. 'Ok, Coco, calm down. I think you might be right, her body's old and her mind is playing tricks on her. I think right now as you say, her home, and you are what's best for her at the moment. Then when she wakes up, she'll be in familiar surroundings. I'll arrange a doctor to call on her. Is there anything else I can do to help you?'

Coco smiled and seemed to relax a bit visibly. 'Please, could you take the cats? There are just too many of them, and I can't fish at the moment with my broken arm. Milking the goats and the other chores is going to be hard enough to manage without all the cats as well.'

Anne said, 'she does have a lot of cats, she has a big heart and does not like to think of anything homeless. Don't worry; I'll take the cats tomorrow. I'll bring some boxes to transport them.'

Anne stayed the rest of the day and helped do the chores; she and Coco took turns on checking Mary, who did not move still or wake up. At four o clock, Anne said, 'I have to go now Coco, it'll be dark soon, and I don't like to row there in the dark. I'll come back tomorrow, with a doctor and boxes for all the cats.'

Coco felt suddenly frightened about being left alone with Mary in such a poor condition. He let out a small huff of air and glanced out the window. He could see one of his boats bobbing along in the water quite close to the shore. Pointing out of the window, he said, 'Anne, please could you help me get the boat back before you leave?' Anne nodded and put on her coat; then the pair got the small boat back.

Coco felt better now that he had a boat, although he could not row because of his broken arm, somehow having it made him not feel so cut off.

Anne was about to cast off her boat and leave for the night, and she noticed how tired and pale Coco looked. 'Are you sure you will be alright, Coco?' she asked again. 'You can change your mind, and I can find someone to help you get Mary back to the mainland.'

Coco sighed and reported that he would be fine. Secretly he was still a little scared to go to the mainland anyway. It was not just the octopus incident that had happened on his only visit, but the small island was all he had come to know.

After Anne had gone, Coco went to sit in Mary's room and read out loud one of her favourite stories in the hope that she could hear him. He did not go into his room that night but fell asleep in a chair next to her bed.

The next day, Anne came back to visit the doctor. When they opened the door to the church, they were greeted by the cats.

'What a lot of cats,' the doctor said.

'Yes, I know, they're all going today,' Anne said. 'I'm pleased to say I've managed to find new homes for them all on the mainland.'

'That's impressive,' said the doctor, admiringly.

'Yes, it wasn't an easy task, but Mary had done a lot of good deeds for many of the people on the mainland so I called in a few favours and reminded a few people of the time she helped them. The house is just through here, Doctor; it's bolted on to the back of the church.'

They walked, through, the doctor briefly stopping to admire the one stained glass window of St Christopher at the far end behind the altar.

Anne and the doctor took their coats off and walked the short way up to Mary's bedroom.

They found Coco still asleep in the chair. Anne quietly showed the doctor Mary, and he started to examine her.

Coco was only in a light, restless sleep, so awoke and was pleased to see the doctor. He didn't talk at once but studied the man from his chair. He was a tall, thin man with a dash of grey hair; he looked old and worldly-wise.

The doctor took out his stethoscope and listened to Mary's heart; he seemed pleased, and as he was putting the instrument back in his bag, he saw Coco looking at him and smiled.

Coco smiled back and asked, 'do you think that she will be ok, doctor?'

'Yes, in time,' he said, reassuringly.

Coco stood up. 'I've been watching her on and off all night, and there's no change. She keeps talking to herself.'

The doctor didn't answer but looked at Coco's arm. 'I have some Plaster-of-Paris, and I'll set that for you in a bit.'

Coco nodded and asked again, in a more worried tone, 'do you think she will be ok now, Doctor?'

The doctor said, 'she does seem stable, but I really think that we should move her to the mainland, were I can keep a better eye on her until she's up and about.'

'No, please let me look after her. I am sure she will get better soon,' Coco said instantly.

'Ok, if you're sure. I can come back in a week's time and check up on her. I know that Anne said she'd come daily until there's an improvement.'

Thank you, Doctor,' Coco said.

'Right then, boy, into the bathroom and I'll set that arm,' he said with a grin.

Coco led the way to the small bathroom, and the doctor mixed some water with the Plaster-of-Paris and dipped bandages in it.

Anne popped her head around the bathroom door and cheerfully said, 'I've brought some boxes to collect the cats.'

The doctor asked, 'are you alright, Anne, to hang on a bit while I finish dressing Coco's arm? Then I will give you a hand to round them all up and load them on the boat.'

Anne said, 'are you sure? There's a lot of them.'

The doctor glanced over at Coco's broken arm. 'Well, he's not going to be doing any loading of boxes with that arm, the plaster needs to set, so it's best I help.'

So started the strange sight of a nun and a doctor trying their best to collect all the cats on the small island.

Anne eventually scooped the last cat into a box, announcing triumphantly, 'that's it, there, all collected!'

Coco said in a shy voice, 'I hope Mary doesn't mind, I mean us getting rid of all her cats.'

The doctor looked at the full boat and said, 'I'm sure she'll understand, I mean there are so many of them, plus Anne has found homes for them all. Now you have a broken arm you can't fish to get their food.' The doctor took a red handkerchief with white polka dots out of his top pocket and wiped the beads of sweat from his forehead. It was exhausting work, cat collecting, he thought to himself. Then he turned to Anne and said, 'I best be getting back now, I some calls to make on the mainland before I start my rounds at the hospital.'

Anne turned to Coco. 'Bye for now. Are you sure that you'll be ok for a bit while I row the doctor back? I'll return at lunch time to help.'

Coco said, 'I'll be fine, thanks. Mary's sleeping now, and I think I'll have a quiet morning sitting with her.'

He waved them off and then made his way up the path to the church, picking some of the small white sweet smelling flowers and herbs to put in a vase by Mary's bed.

Coco spent the morning in Mary's room. He looked out of the window and was pleased to note that the sea was calmer. He went over to sit on the edge of Mary's bed and listened to her breathing; it was strong but shallow. Then at lunch time, he heard a tip-tapping on the corrugated metal roof under Mary's window and was surprised to see hail stones falling from the sky.

'What strange weather,' Coco thought.

A minute later he was relieved to hear Anne dashing in, half laughing with the excitement of it all as she shook off her coat. 'Well I never, whatever next? Hailstones, well, I'm sure it's all in God's plan,' she shouted up from the kitchen.

Coco ran downstairs to greet her and saw that she had already put the kettle on and was laying out some cheese and bread on the table. Anne turned to smile at him. 'How's Mary doing?'

'Much the same,' Coco said, slicing off the end of the loaf of bread and biting into the crust. 'She's still muttering in her sleep, but I can't make out the words.'

Anne looked blankly at him, unsure what to say while making up a small tray and placing a cup of tea and a cheese sandwich for Coco to take up to put on the table by Mary's bed.

When he came back with the empty tray, she said, 'I forgot to ask how your arm is.'

'Oh, it's fine now, hardly hurts at all,' Coco said.

'Let me take a look, will you?

He held his arm out.

Anne looked at Coco's arm. 'The doctor's done a fine job of plastering it, and the fingers don't look so bruised now,' she said, lifting it back carefully into the sling.

'Thanks,' he said, sitting down and sipping the tea.

Just then they heard a weak cry from upstairs, putting down their cups they hurriedly ran upstairs to find Mary sitting up in bed.

Mary looked directly at them. 'Mother?' She asked.

Coco froze in the doorway, and Anne went over and sat by her bed and patted her hand. 'It's Anne, dear,' she said. 'You're fine, you're at home, Coco's here and everything's ok.'

'Water,' she whispered breathlessly, Anne poured a glass of water and held it for her so she could take a sip.

'Thank you,' Mary said, slumping down in her bed and looking around the room, confused.

Coco walked over to stand in front of Mary, but she didn't appear to recognize him. He suddenly felt overwhelmed and upset. He bit back the tears and in panic told Anne he was going to take a walk and see if he could spot the other boat.

Once outside in the fresh air, Coco felt calmer. He walked down the path looking out across the sea for the other boat. He saw a small blue happy-looking boat approach from the direction of the mainland and ran down to the water's edge to welcome it. There was an old man rowing it and a larger lady sitting bolt upright with a steely gaze. Coco recognised her; it was the Mother Superior. Coco caught the rope and looped it over a post on the jetty with his good arm.

The man stepped out of the boat and offered his hand for the Mother Superior to hold as she alighted onto the jetty and greeted Coco with a large smile.

Coco had met the Mother Superior once before; she had walked Mary around to Anne's lodgings after that church service that day on the mainland. He remembered from that time that she liked to ask several questions at once and sometimes did not even wait for an answer.

The Mother Superior placed her hand upon Coco's head as if giving him a blessing, and asked 'how are you, my boy? How's that arm of yours doing?'

'It's a lot better,' Coco said with a small smile.

The old man who had been rowing the boat took a leather tobacco pouch and a clay pipe from his oilskin coat pocket.

Coco studied his face; he must have been seventy years old and had a thin, wiry strength look to him. He had a fat moustache and coughed as he tapped his pipe on the side of the jetty to empty it.

The Mother Superior, picking up her bag and straightening out her clothes, looked at Coco and said, 'Shall we go up now and see the patient? I'm afraid this will be only a short visit, duty calls.

What I want to know is; how she is? Did you know that she was one of my nuns years ago before she decided to leave and come and live on this island?'

Coco led the Mother Superior towards the church, trying to answer as many questions as he could, which she fired off at an impressive speed. As they made their way slowly up the path, Coco stopped and said, 'Thank you for coming to visit us, Mother Superior. Mary is a lot better, her eyes are open, and she's talking, she's just drinking water at the moment, but what's worrying is that she seems not to know where she is or even who I am. 'This led to another barrage of questions and then the Mother Superior turned to look at Coco and could see that he was getting overly concerned so changed the subject.

'Tell me, my boy, how did you break that arm of yours? You know I used to be a nurse before I was a nun, I will look at it later if you like.'

'There's no need, the doctor has already fixed it,' Coco said defensively. He did not like all the fuss about his arm when poor Mary was obviously so ill.

Mother Superior opened the door to the church and smiled at the interior. It was a very lovely old stone building with ancient plaster on the walls that had been decorated with fleur-de-lis stencilling. She ran her hand along the polished wooden pews and over the rustic stone font and sniffed the large old leather-bound Bible on the altar. 'It's pleasant here, I can see why Mary chose to stay,' she said while nodding her head in agreement with herself.

Coco gestured the way, and the Mother Superior followed him up the small staircase to Mary's room.

When she got into the room, Anne said, 'Mother Superior!' and jumped up from the chair so that she could sit down.

Mary was asleep again, and Mother Superior walked over to the bed and placed a hand on Mary's forehead. 'Her head feels hot, I think she may have a temperature,' she said in a loud, indignant voice and, turning to Coco, she said, 'I really think you should both come back with me where there is access to a doctor.'

Coco groaned. 'The doctor has done his checks and is happy for her to stay here, plus Anne is coming daily at the moment to help.'

'Well, I guess that's ok if this is what the doctor recommends,' Mother Superior said, glancing at Anne to get her approval.

Anne nodded curtly. 'Tea, Mother Superior?'

The Mother Superior smiled and said, 'just a quick cup, I have to get back to my flock.'

They all walked down the stairs and into the kitchen. As Anne poured the tea, they all sat at the kitchen table, looking blankly at each other.

After a few minutes had passed and the Mother Superior had drained her second cup of tea, she asked to speak privately to Anne. They got up from the table and went into the side room, which had the old piano and some boxes in it. 'So,' Mother Superior started, carefully closing the door behind them and using a hushed tone, 'it's just been the two of them all these years?'

Anne looked a bit nervous. 'Yes, just the two of them, apart from all of the cats, that is, but they've been managing well and have been very self-sufficient. Mary has taught Coco all his schooling, he's a bright boy, brighter than most and they care for each other very much.'

The Mother Superior replied in a worried tone, 'I'm not sure this is the right environment for a young boy. I've known Mary for many years now, and I think she was always a little crazy, but now she appears to be losing it completely. Tell me, who are the boy's parents?'

Anne looked at the floor, not sure how to explain the situation. She nervously said, 'well, um, Coco doesn't appear to have any parents. Mary found him one morning washed up on a mat of seaweed by the jetty. She believed he was a gift from God; you know like Moses and the bed of reeds.'

The Mother Superior looked shocked, so Anne continued, 'He's a bit different, you know, not quite like a normal boy, he has these strange tube-like things at the back of his neck. Mary thought that whoever had put him on that seaweed mat didn't want a freak as a child, so had set him adrift.'

Mother Superior had a serious look on her face and said, 'Still, he's a young boy, and she's an eccentric old cat lady. I'm not sure she's the right influence for a child. Surely he would be better off in the orphanage run by the church on the mainland.'

Anne said, 'at first I had my doubts, but I've watched them over the years, and I don't feel that Coco could have had a happier childhood. He's safe here and loved.'

The Mother Superior smiled. 'God works in mysterious ways, let's hope Mary recovers and things can return to normal for them both. Anne, shall we have a short prayer together for them before I leave?'

They walked back out of the room, Coco had returned upstairs, so the Mother Superior shouted a cheery goodbye, and the two nuns went into the church to pray and then made their way home.

This went on for six weeks. Anne visited daily, and the doctor came now and then, and the Mother Superior made an occasional visit. Anne did all the nursing, washing Mary and changing her bed sheets. Coco did his best to stay on top of the chores and tend the goats.

It was after another hailstorm that Anne called up to the house for her normal visit and was shocked to see that the church door was open and swinging in the wind. She could sense in the air that there was something wrong, everything quieter than normal. She quickened her pace and raced up the path, dropping her shopping bags as she went.

She shouted Coco's name as she made her way quickly through the church to the house at the back. She got no answer, so hurried upstairs to Mary's room, only to find that Mary's covers were all on the floor, and there was no sign of her.

She raced outside. On the highest cliff edge, she saw a limp body slumped, peering down into the sea, sitting motionless.

'Coco!' Anne shouted, walking slowly towards the boy so that she did not startle him.

Coco did not look up; his bloodshot eyes were fixed on the jagged rocks below and the swells of the water.

Anne went over and, taking off her coat, wrapped it around his shoulders. Coco was shivering and white as a ghost, ice cold.

'How long of you been out here? Where's Mary?'

Coco could not speak at first; he just pointed to the jagged rocks below.

'Oh,' said Anne in a worried tone. 'What happened?'

Coco started crying. 'Last night she seemed quite at peace, so I went to bed in my room. I was in a deep sleep as the last few weeks have been exhausting. I had not meant to sleep so deeply.

'Then something woke me up; I'm not sure what and there was Mary standing over my bed, staring at me. She looked like she didn't recognize me, then she ran back out the door.

'I pulled my senses together and chased after her. She ran to this cliff and stood with her back to the edge.

'I'd nearly caught up to her when she just fell backwards on the rocks, the waves came and took her body under almost immediately.

'I knew there was nothing I could do. If I had got the boat out and tried to row with my one good arm, it would have taken me a whole hour to get around to this point under the cliffs. The sea's rough and the tide was going out; her body would have been long gone.'

Anne put her arm around him and held him close. 'Oh Coco you mustn't distress yourself, there was nothing you could have done. Come back into the house and get some sleep, we'll think about what needs to be done.'

Coco stopped crying; he was exhausted and cold, he got up slowly and followed Anne back towards the church. However, he felt that he would not be able to sleep as every time he closed his eyes he a vision of Mary falling onto the rocks. Eventually, tiredness took over his young body and, in the end; he did sleep, and when he awoke, he found his things packed for him and Mother Superior told him he was told he would be taken care of at the orphanage.

Coco was not happy. 'What about the goats?' he cried, glaring at a red faced Anne.

The Mother Superior patted him on the head. 'They'll be taken to the mainland. Everything belongs to the church now; this is what happened when a nun dies.' Coco started to pull his things out of his bag, and Anne went over to talk to him.

'Look, Coco I know it's a shock, but when a lady becomes a nun they give all their worldly possessions to the church, it's the way it has always been. They can carry on living in the houses if they choice but when they die everything reverts to the church by law.'

Coco did not understand; he glared at the Mother Superior. She averted her eyes from his stare and settled back into packing up Mary's things into cardboard boxes.

As they got down to the small boat waiting to take Coco away from his home forever, he turned back and looked up towards the church, making a silent promise to himself that one day he would return to the island, buy it and live there again.

Chapter 3

(Arm 3).

Time for Change

The orphanage was a large, intimidating old building made from dull red bricks. It had a lifeless clinical feel about it, the only movement being the large minute hand on the modern white faced clock incorporated high up in the brickwork. At the entrance were imposing black wrought iron gates which squeaked noisily as they blew in the wind. Coco pulled the collar of his coat around his neck tightly to cover his tubes as he was ushered in through the gates. He looked about him; there was a small garden as such, a few shrubs and bare soil which had been carefully hemmed in by red brick edging stones in a wavy style. A small path led up to some grand glass doors.

As they entered through them, they were met in the reception by a middle-aged stern looking lady wearing yellow lensed spectacles. She threw Coco a small thin smile as they entered and Anne handed her a letter. After the initial welcome, Coco was taken to the first floor in the building and shown into a dormitory full of boys of similar age to him. He was assigned bed linen, pyjamas and three white towels which had the orphanage name sewn on them in green piping and given the bed next the window.

Coco was not pleased as the window was small and he started to feel panicky and caged like a trapped animal. He stood on tiptoes and peered out, looking at the sea in the distance. He longed to be out on one of his boats in the fresh air, far away, sailing into the sunset and catching fish. His thoughts turned again to Mary; his small heart ached with emptiness and knew that he would never forget her.

Anne went over to Coco and tapped him on his shoulder, jerking Coco momentarily from his daze. 'I have to go now, but I'll call back shortly and see how you're settling in.'

Coco swung around and gave Anne a blank look, then returned his gaze to the window and his thoughts to sailing far away.

In the room behind him, Coco could hear the other boys sniggering and pointing at him.

'Look at that boy's long hair,' one of them said.

'Maybe it's a girl,' another jeered.

The larger one stood up and roughly tugged Coco's hair at the back of his head and pointed at the tubes. In a taunting voice he said, 'That, not a girl, it's a freak! Look, he's just using his hair to hide weird freaky tubes things at the back of his neck. That's why he's here; his parents didn't want a freak tube boy for a child!'

All the boys started calling him 'tube boy' under their breath at first, and then the chant got louder and louder until it filled the room and was deafening. Coco tried to ignore them and turned his gaze to look out of the window once more.

The larger boy threw a book at him, and the others laughed.

Coco was angry. He lunged at the boy, and an inky black substance dripped from the tips of his fingers.

'Err! What's that?' the boy shouted, recoiling in disgust.

Coco shot out of the room and locked himself in the bathroom, where he collapsed on the floor, sobbing.

He didn't want to be in the orphanage, he felt different and wanted to go back to his island, he wanted Mary to still be alive. He started to cry harder, his whole body shuddering. Coco closed his eyes tightly to try and shut the world out but each time he did, he saw flashes of images that replayed in his mind of Mary falling backwards onto the cliffs, her small, fragile body hitting the waves and disappearing from his view forever. He had never felt such sadness in his young life as he did at that point; he wasn't even sure if he wanted to live anymore or was even able to.

After a while, there was a quiet knock on the door. 'Coco?' Anne called out softly, peering through the frosted glass. 'Let me in, my dear boy, so we can talk.' She started to rattle the handle.

Coco pulled himself up and lunged towards the door. As he opened it, Anne threw her arms around him and drew him to her chest, hugging him.

'I miss Mary so much, Anne, 'Coco sobbed, biting back the fear caused by the emptiness in his heart.

'I know, I know, she was my best friend too and the kindest person in the world,' Anne said in a soft voice as she stroked Coco's long curly hair.

Coco looked down at his hands covered with the inky black substance. 'What's up with me? Am I a freak?'

Anne took a clean flannel from the sink and bathed and dried Coco's hands tenderly. It was then that she handed Coco a book. 'This is Mary's journal; she wanted you to have it. In it are detailed records of all of your days together and every happy memory you shared.'

Coco took the journal. It was a medium sized leather bound book with cream pages. Every page contained carefully written small joined up writing. Scattered amongst the pages was a collection of loose photographs and pencil drawings.

Anne hugged Coco again and said, 'You are God's creature, Coco, you are not a freak, just different. I know you feel alone and scared right now, but you mustn't worry, child, come with me to see the doctor; he has a plan that will make you normal.'

Coco splashed some water on his face and looked at himself in the mirror. He knew he was not normal, but he was angry and hurt by the other children's actions and thought if that was normal he didn't want any part of it.

Anne took Coco by the hand and led him past the other now quite remorseful children and down the long corridor.

In the school nurse's room, the doctor was waiting behind a large white painted desk. He smiled at Coco as he came in, but Coco did not feel comforted by this. His eyes scanned the room; he could see all manner of machinery, boxes with large clockwork dials and instruments that looked like they belonged on robots or a space ship. A collection of sharp knives and scalpels were also on display in a padlocked glass case. Coco shuddered at the sight of them.

The doctor walked over and looked at the plaster cast on his arm. 'Anne tells me this cast has been on for six weeks now, so it's time to cut it off, as your arm will be healed.'

The doctor took a small brass key from his pocket and opened the padlocked glass cabinet where he chose a pair of odd shaped scissors and started to snip carefully along the cast. Coco could not watch, but soon it was over, and Coco was relieved to have his arm back again.

Next the doctor briefly examined the tubes on the back of his neck. Then he said, 'Don't worry, child, we can operate and take the tubes off you and then you will look normal, like the other children.'

Coco suddenly became very scared. 'No!' he shouted.

Anne went over and put her arm around Coco's shoulders in a comforting way, then spoke softly to him. 'Look, it's for the best. The operation's all set for tomorrow, the doctor will give you some medication in your food, and then you will slip into a nice sleep and he can cut the tubes away, and you will be like everyone else.'

Everyone else. The words rang through Coco's head and echoed in his ears.

Anne was stroking his hand, but Coco could not stop shivering. 'No,' he said again, 'I'm sure I wouldn't like that.'

Anne patted his hand. 'Well, I know it's a new idea, and you're probably not up to thinking about it all just yet so close after losing Mary; Just sleep on it.'

The doctor walked back to his desk, scribbled down a few notes, then looked up and said, 'Anne, can you take him to back his room now, please?'

Coco turned white and shook slightly. 'I don't want to go back there; the other boys are mean.'

Anne looked concerned and said, 'it's ok, Coco, there's an empty bedroom at the top of the building, I use it sometimes for meditation. It's in the attic, it's a bit cold but nice, I keep a bed made up ready. You will be alone and quiet, that could be your room for a while if you would like, but first come and have your meal with the other children and then you will be set up until the morning.'

Coco nodded, and Anne showed him the way to the large dining room, which doubled as a school gym. They collected a small wooden tray each and joined the long queue of excited children. When it was their turn, they selected a shepherd's pie each, which Anne explained was minced beef with peas and carrots topped with mashed potatoes. There was a range of puddings to choice from, but they both chose a steamed treacle pudding with custard.

The meal smelt wonderful, and Anne sat with Coco at one of the long wooden tables, which had large metal jugs with water in and short fat glasses.

After the meal, they took their trays over to the kitchen so the plates could be washed up and Anne showed Coco up to the attic room. As they walked through the building, Coco looked about him. It was a strange place, there were twisty staircases and long dimly gas lit hallways, with many dormitories running off them. There was loud chattering amongst the children coming from behind the heavy doors, and as Coco and Anne passed them all, he felt pleased he would not have to face the other boys in the orphanage again for a while.

After walking along many corridors and climbing a lot of staircases, they came to the highest part of the building. This was reached by a long metal open stairway, which spiralled up to the top and came out at the back of the clock. Coco looked in wonder at the translucent white clock face as they passed it, he could see the minute hand moving and the cogs and clockwork workings, spinning and whirling at the back.

Anne took out a large bunch of keys as they reached the door and carefully opened it. A rush of cold air greeted them. She hurried over to shut the small window and then opened an old wardrobe and took out a thick wool blanket. She shook it out and placed it on top of the three existing blankets on the small single iron framed bed.

'There,' she announced triumphantly. Coco looked around the small room; it had old dusty tea chests with the brand names of tea stamped on them.

Anne pointed to a small door in the far corner, 'that's a bathroom through there, with towels and soap.'

Coco half smiled, and Anne hugged him once more, then left him alone with his thoughts.

Coco was pleased to be in a room on his own. He examined the tea chests and studied an old photo of a steam engine operating a crane lifting the glass clock face into the top of the building. Then he explored the tiny bathroom before returning to sit on the bed with his back propped up against the wall. He had a cushion and settled himself down so he could start to read Mary's journal. Everything was so quiet this high up in the building apart from the rush of the wind against the window pane and the heavy and constant tick of the large clock.

He carefully opened the journal and read every small detail, all about his life, how he was found, how Mary believed he was a gift from God and how she felt that God had made him in a special way for a reason, and he should be proud of that difference. Mary must have meant for him to read all this and so had recorded every tiny detail from every day since he washed up on the beach to the last entry, moments before she had become ill. It was a comfort to read it. Mary had loved him more than anyone in her whole long and rich life, and her words gave such relief that tears streamed down Coco's face as he read her kind soft words about their lives together. Suddenly he began not to feel so alone anymore.

Coco read all night, and when he got to the last page, his eyes were overflowing with tears, and his heart was full. He felt sad but also happy that he had spent fifteen years of his life with such a beautiful person. Coco felt that Mary had given him a gift, the gift of wisdom; he felt she was wise, that she had possessed a rich knowledge and was a gifted writer. He knew that everyone else felt that she had been a mad old cat lady and a religious nut, he knew different and in the dimness of that tiny room this was an overwhelming comfort to him.

Mary had been an inspiration and, more than ever, he felt it was fated that she had found and cared for him. She had not wanted to change him like the doctor at the orphanage, or judged him to be different like all the mean boys. She had been the opposite and celebrated Coco for who he was.

He had only been in the orphanage for a few hours, but already he hated it and did not want to stay and he certainly did not trust the doctor. The more Coco thought about it, the more he became paranoid. How could I eat anything else? he thought. There could be a chance that the food may be drugged. He understood that the staff believed what they were doing was the right by letting the doctor operate on him, cutting away his tubes to make him look like everyone else. In that moment, Coco knew that he had to escape, but how?

He had heard Anne turn the key in the lock, so he knew he could not go through the door. He walked to the window, it was barred, the bars too close together for him to squeeze through, or were they? Now he was about to discover another gift that he had; this would not be the last.

Coco climbed onto a chair so that he could reach the barred window. He pushed his head against the bars and tapped it gingerly. Then, to his shock, his head started to change shape, narrow from the top. It was as if he had willed himself to be thinner. Slowly he pushed his head through the narrow bars and then edged his shoulders, though, finally his torso and legs.

Once out on the roof, Coco caught his breath and stared back at the bars, barely believing what had happened. He looked around him; he was high up, and it looked even higher now he was outside and looking down. Quickly he leaned back into the room and grabbed the leather journal. This was now his most precious persecution.

He tucked it into the top of his trousers for safe keeping and scoured the roof top for a way to escape down to the street below.

All was quiet, not a soul about, presumably as it was the early hours of the morning and it would have been fully dark if it was not for the light of the moon.

It was a full moon. Its golden light shone down and lit up the street with an eerie glow.

Coco spied a small flat roof just below the main roof at the end. He moved along it. He had not been this high before, but somehow he was not afraid; he crept to the edge and lowered himself down onto it.

There was a small staircase which led just under the white clock face and down into a back alley. When he got down to the ground, he suddenly became aware of his dire situation. What was he to do? He had no money and no possessions other than the clothes on his back and his precious journal.

He was feeling cold and wished he had brought his coat. He hesitated a moment while thinking whether he should attempt to go back to claim it.

He knew it would get colder but suddenly felt panic-stricken, so he walked on.

He strode along to the small jetty where brightly coloured boats wobbled in welcome. He thought about rowing back out to his island and living there, but he knew it would be almost impossible to row with his arm fresh out of plaster, plus the doctor and Anne would look there first for him. Also, he knew that his island home now belonged to the church and his hope of sanctuary there was lost.

He must have walked for two hours; he was feeling cold and tired. He ducked into a shop doorway to rest and stooped down, hugging himself. The wind howled past with a cold chill, blowing leaves into a rustling heap next to him, but the shop doorway gave just enough protection to stop its bite.

Coco looked about him. On the shop door was a brightly coloured poster that said, circus. It had a drawing of an elephant waving a flag. The colours were happy, and inviting, and the elephant looked jolly. Coco had read about the circus in one of Mary's books and had always thought that one day he would like to see it and now in some sort of hopeful dream, he imagined that there might be a chance of some work, maybe even feeding the elephant.

He heard the rattling noise of a horse and cart rumbling along the cobbled street. He peered around the corner and, to his horror saw the doctor and Anne approaching in it, slowly scouring the street. He heard Anne calling his name.

Coco felt himself go white with fear; he froze on the spot. They were almost upon him; there was nowhere he could run, and he felt sure that he would be seen if he moved from the doorway. Fear burned up in his stomach and cramped in his chest. He knew that if they got him, they would make him go back; he did not want to go; he knew that they were going to force him into having that operation. Sweat fell from his brow, although he was really too cold to sweat.

Sickness began to form in his mouth. Nearer and nearer along the road they came, the noise of the wooden wheels on the cobbles rumbling louder and louder and Anne's voice intensifying, so it echoed all around him. Coco's breathing became shallower as he knew that one or two seconds was all he had before they would see him and then all hope would be lost.

His heart was thumping hard in his chest, and he felt his whole body shaking. He had learned about 'fight or flight' mode from Mary's books and guessed that he must be in flight mode.

But then something magical happened. As the horse and cart went past the shop doorway, the doctor looked directly at Coco but appeared not to see him.

Coco held his breath and stood motionless. Thoughts raced through his head, how could that be? How could the doctor not see him? After all, he was staring right at him. He knew they were looking for him, Anne was calling his name.

Shaking with shock and adrenalin, Coco looked at his reflection in the shop window and gasped.

He had camouflaged; his face, body, arms and legs were a brickwork pattern which matched the wall behind. Even Coco's clothes appeared to have the same pattern. Shocked, he reached down and touched the sleeve of his jumper to see the pattern shimmer and quiver as if it was a mass of jelly.

Again Coco's breathing became shallower, and he started to return to normal. He felt slightly drained of energy as he gazed at the brightly coloured poster of the circus attached opposite him on the glass door of the shop. He decided there and then that he would go to the circus. For comfort's sake, again he playfully imagined himself working there, feeding the elephants and being happy. However, as it turned out feeding the elephants was not all that was fated or in store for him.

Coco read the poster carefully to work out where the circus was set up. It was quite a hike, but he felt happy and full of purpose as he set off towards it. He must have been walking all morning, he was cold and thirsty and stopped to drink water from a flowing stream and then rested a while on the grassy bank. He looked up the road and could see people travelling by horse and cart, chatting merrily, heading in the direction of the circus. He set off again and as he got closer he walked amongst the crowds of smiling people and excited children.

Coco's heart raced when he got his first glimpse of the top of the circus tent. It was a huge structure, red with white stripes and long flags high above it, flapping in welcome in the wind. From the loud music, he could tell that the show was about to start, and he hurried towards it. Not having any money, he waited until a large group of children were going in and slipped in amongst them.

He took a seat on the second row from the back and felt really excited.

The Ringmaster entered the ring brandishing a whip in one hand and a megaphone in the other. He was a short, stout man. His jet black hair which was slicked back on both sides with a middle parting and shone like a raven's wing. On his chubby face, he sported fine bushy sideburns that he had brushed up so much that they looked fluffy.

He wore a tight-fitting white shirt with a button on collar, a bow tie, a long bright red jacket which matched his tight fitting trousers. His feet seemed very small, but his tiny boots were shined brightly, and he had a grin reminiscent of a Cheshire cat.

From the side of the circus ring a trumpet sounded a salute and then the Ring Master shouted through his megaphone, 'Ladies and gentlemen, welcome to the most amazing experience of your life!

'We have gathered acts from across the globe for your entertainment. We have Mack the Magnificent, a swordsman, archer and juggler extraordinaire. Mack will be walking a tightrope while juggling swords blindfolded.'

Everyone gasped as Mack shot out into the ring riding a brown and white horse and fired three flaming arrows at a target a pretty girl held up. Next, Mack jumped off the horse and started juggling his swords high into the air and then took a bow.

The Ringmaster said, 'we have Mack's wife, Michelle, who is a real mermaid from the deepest part of the ocean, who Mack enchanted with his singing.' The Ringmaster pointed toward the open tent flaps just as six white horses with long manes and plaited tails came out pulling a golden carriage with a large globe shape tank on it. This was highly decorated with golden leaves, flowers and sea shells. Inside Coco could see a lady with long brown hair and a beautiful long metallic tail which contained all the colours of the rainbow. She dived into the water and peered out of the sides of her bowl through her fingers at everyone in the audience as the carriage travelled slowly around the ring.

Next a youngish man, dressed all in black, ran out into the ring, sparks flying about him. 'Ladies and Gentlemen, welcome Eric, the Electric Magician.'

Eric took a bow.

Next the Ringmaster pointed above him. The crowd stood up and roared as the spotlight fell on a beautiful woman with long hair dressed in an emerald green tutu covered in sparkling jewels. She was swinging high in the rafters hanging upside down, so her long hair flowed down below her.

The drums sounded, and the Ringmaster announced, 'The first act is a death-defying trapeze act, Megan the Great, who is the sensation of the ages. She will swing and attempt a triple spin without the aid of her net. But this is not all as at the same time above Megan will be a balancing act by Mack the Magnificent! He will juggle his swords blindfolded on the tightrope.'

The band struck up a tune and Coco watched in wonder as Mack ran along the tightrope throwing three swords high in the air and catching them all with ease. Then Mack took off his blindfold and climbed down to stand opposite where Megan swung back and forth on her trapeze swing which was decorated in lilac coloured flowers. She started to swing faster; her long hair flowed behind her, and the crowd gasped at the spectacle of it all. Then she performed a single spin trapeze jump, and then a double spin trapeze jump and then the drums sounded and the nets were taken down. The spotlight went back onto Megan as she built up speed in her swing. The crowd looked up, hardly daring to breathe. Coco was amazed when they took the net down, as to perform such a dangerous trick with no form of safety seemed so dangerous. He could not bear to watch; she would surely die if Mack missed catching her.

Faster and faster Megan swung, the drums rolled, and then she jumped and spun three times. It was as if time stood still for a moment and people's hearts had stopped beating. A silence hit the crowd and Coco were sure he could hear Megan's heart racing, but at last as she came out of the final spin and was caught firmly by Mack. Everyone cheered, and Coco only looked up again when he heard the children cheering and clapping. Then underneath the pair, several clowns dashed out, and there was more juggling. Mack swung down into the middle of the ring where one of the clowns handed him some flaming batons which he threw high into the air and then, touching one of the batons to his mouth, breathed out fire. Coco thought this was the most amazing thing he had ever seen.

The juggling act finished and next came some the performing dogs that run around and jumped over the clowns, knocking them over and making all the children laugh. The clowns and dogs ran off again.

The band struck up a happy song; the Ringmaster came into the ring and pointed to the band. The music stopped abruptly, and the Ringmaster went to the centre stage. The white horses charged around the ring wearing beautiful plumes and bowing their heads gracefully.

Next came the elephant act. Coco was very excited, seeing the elephants was the main reason he had wanted to come to the circus, as he had only seen them in books. Coco watched the act and was transfixed. There were three elephants which were much larger than he had imagined. They had long big ears, and each waved a flag and balanced their two front feet on a ball.

The Ringmaster cracked his whip. The elephant trainer carried a long pole with a heavy metal lump on one end and a shaped spike on the other. The trainer followed the elephants around, and if they did not do what he wanted quickly enough, he jabbed them hard with the spike.

The elephants jerked and moved quickly to do as they were told.

He got one elephant to sit down and one to sit on it.

Then he got them all to put their front legs on each other and walk out the ring.

Everyone cheered, but Coco did not like the act now that he was close up and could see the sadness in the elephants' eyes so many times.

Next came the young man dressed in black came out and everyone clapped. The Ringmaster shouted through his megaphone, 'welcome Eric, the Electrical Act!' Eric moved into the centre of the ring wearing a top hat and a long black cape. The lights were turned down, and great flashes started to shoot out in all directions around him. Then Eric pointed to his robot, he circled it and then, taking off his cape, threw it over the robot. Eric stood in front of the robot and took off his hat. Flashes shot around the tent. Seconds later Eric stepped aside, and the cape was on the floor, and the robot was gone. There was a drum roll and the spotlight shone around the arena until it stopped on the rigging where the trapeze artist was before. There was the robot. The crowd gasped, Coco gasped. Eric bowed and backed out of the ring, creating electrical flashes around the room. It was spectacular.

Everyone clapped. Then the clowns come out, rolling around squeaking horns and throwing pretend water at each other. Everyone roared with laughter.

The Ringmaster announced, 'now we have the fabulous Moss brothers, Will and Bob, who will saw their assistant, Lady Jane, in half.' Two identical dashingly good looking men wearing brown pinstriped suits and bowler hats with goggles walked into the ring, both holding a lady's hand. She was wearing a pinstriped skirt and jacket suit and had large feathers in her pink hair. All three were smiling and waved to everyone as the clowns set up their equipment behind them.

The audience gasped as Will held up the large saw and walked around the ring with it. Bob held Jane's hand and helped her into the large coffin-shaped box. The lights dimmed, and a drum roll began. As Will started to saw though the coffin-shaped box, Bob wiped his brow for him with a large polka dot hanky. The noise of the sawing vibrated around the tent. Some children started to cry, and one lady fainted with the excitement of it all. Finally, the drum beat stopped, and a silence travelled around the audience and the two twin brothers unclipped the coffin shaped box and spun the two halves around in a circle. Next they clipped the two halves of the box back together and then Will dramatically waved his hand over Jane. Nothing, no movement, the crowd gasped and then Bob leaned down and listened to see if she was breathing and gently gave her a small kiss on her lips. Jane's eyes opened, and a huge smile washed over her face, reflecting in Bob's eyes. Will hurriedly opened the lid and Bob took Jane's hand and helped her from the box. They all stood in front and took a bow.

Then, as if by magic the woman who had fainted came to, the children stopped crying, and everyone all clapped as they realized it was a trick.

Coco had just got over the shock of that act when a knife thrower started throwing knives into a board at a pretty blindfolded lady.

After that act was over the freaks came out, the bearded lady, the Siamese twins, the tattooed lady, the fat man, the tall man, the short man, everyone and every size you can imagine and finally the last act was the fat lady singing.

Everyone clapped and cheered. The acts came out and took a bow, and the horses pulled the mermaid's tank around the ring one last time. Mack swung from the rafters with a sword in his teeth.

The Ringmaster walked around the ring once and then the band struck up, and everybody left the tent.

The show was over. Coco desperately looked around for someone to talk to so he could ask about a job. He saw the elephant handler and approached him.

'Please, sir,' Coco said shyly, 'I want to join your circus and help feed the elephants.'

The man laughed. 'You and every other child,' he said as he walked off.

Then Coco saw the Ringmaster sitting on an elephant stand wiping his brow with a white handkerchief. Coco admired his red-tailed suit, his black top hat and whispy bushy sideburns.

He went up to him. 'Please sir, I enjoyed your show, I have nowhere to go, and I would like to join your circus. I'll work hard and not be a problem.'

The Ringmaster turned to look and smiled. 'We have no work for you here. We're special people; you need to be special if you want to be in the circus. What can you do? Go away, ordinary boy.'

Coco was about to walk away when the pretty girl who was in the act of the knife thrower, said, 'Wait, give him a chance. What can you do, boy?'

Coco was not sure he could trust them, but the girl smiled at him and patted him on the back.

'He looks a special boy to me, give him a chance! Go on boy, sing or something,' she said encouragingly, to Coco.

The Ringmaster glared at him.

Coco took a breath and squashed himself through the small gap in the elephant's stool while the Ringmaster was still sat on it.

The Ringmaster jumped up, shocked. 'Oh my God! I don't believe my eyes! What else can you do, lad?'

'I can change, so I merge into the background. However, these are new skills; it was only today realized I had them.'

The pretty girl pointed to suckers at the back of Coco's neck. 'Err, what are those?'

Coco brushed his hair over to try and cover his suckers and said, 'I was born with them, from what I can tell I was born out at sea.'

The girl, undeterred by Coco's attempts to hide the suckers, leaned over and touched them. They wriggled under her touch and sent tingles down Coco's spine. 'Err, this looks like an octopus,' she said, disgusted.

The Ringmaster laughed. 'That's it!' he said, 'we'll call him Octopus Boy. Lad, welcome to the circus.' He held out his fat hand and grabbed Coco's hand in a warm handshake, saying, 'to begin with you can just help out around the place until we've worked out your act. The girl will show you to your lodgings; you'll have to share with the other special people.'

'He means freaks,' the pretty girl laughed.

Coco didn't mind; he felt he was safe, at least for now, with people that he could fit in with.

He was given a grand welcome at the tent where the performers slept. He looked around at all the happy smiles. Then he spotted Michelle, the mermaid, who was now out of the water and sat in a chair. She waved at Coco, and he ran over to admire her tail.

Mack, the sword juggler, greeted Coco and bent down to shake his hand. 'Hello and welcome,' he said in a genuine way.

Coco looked up at Mack. He was much taller now that he was up close, but Coco was not scared and said, 'hello, sir, I admired your act. Please tell me, how are you able to catch the swords when you are blindfolded?'

Mack appeared humbled by Coco's words. 'I have unusual hearing, it's real sensitive. I can pick up sounds that most normal humans can't hear, but mostly it's just practice. I practice as much as I can, sometimes up to eight hours a day. As you're coming to join us in our merry band here, I can teach you about swords and juggling and fighting as well, if you like.'

Coco nodded his head, quite stunned by Mack's friendliness and kindness. Then he walked around the tent and spoke to everyone, showing his tubes at the back of his neck and telling them of the new act that he would be performing. They admired him for being different and didn't poke fun at him. Coco was given some bedding and shown where to bed down for the night. He was very tired as he had not slept properly for a while. He hurriedly laid out his bedding and rested on top of it, closing his eyes. But he could not sleep as he felt too full of adrenalin caused by the extraordinary day's events, so he waited until everyone had settled for the night and then snuck out, determined to find the elephants.

Coco was curious about the elephants and had been upset to see the sadness in their eyes. It was not long before he found the enclosure where the elephants where bedded down for the night. He was worried that they might be asleep but was relieved to see that they were still awake. Coco held his hand out to the nearest one in the same way as he used to when he was feeding Mary's goats. The elephant bowed its head and stared Coco in the eye.

Coco wished he had something to feed then with. He quickly scanned the tent and saw a barrel of apples in a small cage on the far side. They won't miss a few, he thought, and ran over, opened the cage and took three apples out. He presented them to the elephants who took them in their trunks and then put them into their mouths.

While they were crunching them, Coco went over and patted the elephants' rough skin.

'Hello, girls,' he said. 'I'm hoping we can be friends. I don't have a real friend in the world, and you look like a nice friend to have.'

The elephants walked over to the caged apples.

Coco laughed. 'Well, I guess one each more won't hurt.' He opened the cage, took another three apples out and gave one each to each of the elephants. They seemed pleased and walked over to their bedding area to stand and eat them.

'You're clever old things, aren't you?' Coco said affectionately, stroking the elephants again.

Coco noticed that there seemed sadness still in their eyes, so he spoke softly to them and stroked them each again.

He had seen in Mary's books where elephants came from; they lived in big open space along with lots of other elephants. He thought the elephants must be as sad as he had felt being cooped up in that orphanage.

He stayed a while and then started to walk back when he saw sparks flying from a nearby tent. Curious, he went over and peered into the tent. It was the young man, Eric, who had been in the electrical act. He was working on an intricate machine of brass and wood and had small pulses of electrical green and yellow light flashing around it. Eric had a brown leather apron on and goggles; he was holding a soldering iron and attaching a glass bulb.

Coco went in and introduced himself. 'Hello, I'm new here. I watched your act, and I'm really impressed with your trick.'

'It's not a trick, it's all real,' the man retorted.

'Wow!' said Coco. 'In that case, it's, even more, amazing. Um, what are you building now?'

'I'm building a new part of my act, but I don't have all the parts yet to finish it. They cost a lot of money, and the circus doesn't pay much.'

Coco was really excited. 'Well, if you let me come and help you build it, you can keep any money I get from my act when I perform it.'

Eric smiled. 'Let me get this straight: you'll come and help me each evening, and you'll give me all your money for parts.'

Coco nodded.

'Deal!' he said, smiling. 'My name's Eric.'

'I'm Coco,' Coco said. 'Please, Eric, can I ask you one more question about your act? I mean, if it's not a trick and it's all real, how do you do it? Make the robot disappear from one side of the tent and re-appear on the other side?'

'How do you think?' Eric challenged him.

'Well,' said Coco, 'I was watching you really closely, and I have to say that I'm not sure, maybe there are two robots, and you use a sleight of hand or mirrors or something.'

'Ha, ha, not even close,' Eric, beamed at him. 'The trick is that there is no trick.'

Coco looked blankly at Eric.

Eric gave a broad smile. 'I've learned how to teleport the robot from one side of the tent to the other. Also, I can send the robot back in time, for just a few minutes.'

'Wow, time travel,' Coco said. 'They are always my favourite books to read, after the pirate stories that is, wow, amazing!'

Eric smiled and then in a sombre voice said, 'that it is, Coco; that it is. We must both get some rest now as it's always an early start to the day for the life of a circus worker.'

In the weeks that followed, Coco practiced his act, and he and Eric became the best of friends. Mack taught both Coco and Eric how to handle a blade. Coco was a natural. Eric loved sword fighting, he and Mack were about the same age and had mock battles, swinging at each other from across the rafters of the tent, swords clashing and screaming at the top of their voices, 'Yar!' and other pirate talk.

The circus toured around the country on its set route, mostly travelling at night by steam train. The circus owned its own train, brightly painted red and green and had amazing sculptures and mirrored wagons designed to reflect light and dazzle in the sunlight along the sides.

However, as it was a big effort and slow to move with all the equipment they needed, so there were also horse drawn carriages that would often set off a day ahead to make all the preparations for the next show ground.

On this occasion, Mack and Coco went ahead, and Coco used the opportunity of the long slow trip to get to know Mack more. The pair talked nonstop all that day until they got to the showground where the circus would set up the next day. Mack unharnessed one of the horses and rode into the town to arrange everything, such as supplies, and sorted out posters out to be printed.

Meanwhile, Coco set up camp, made a fire and put a pot of stew on to cook. There was a lovely clear sky that evening and by the time Mack arrived back, the fire was going a treat, and the stew was cooked to perfection. Mack fed and watered the horses, then threw his bag down and was pleased to be immediately handed a plate of hot stew and a mug of sweet milky tea. The meal was delicious, and they quickly finished it.

After Coco had cleared the plates away, Mack took out his guitar and started to play the most beautiful and magical song. He sang the notes so clear and pure that tears began to flow down Coco's cheeks, and he could not understand why. It was as if it touched a memory that was lost inside him, perhaps from when his mother had first held him or even when the octopus that he had rescued that day had touched his arm, and he had felt connected to it.

After the song, Coco said slowly 'Mack, you have a real gift with your voice and music.'

Mack smiled and looked up at the stars. Coco had been taught about the stars by Mary and Mack also had studied them and knew how to navigate by them. He pointed up and said, 'that's my home that way, it's the way to America. That's where I'm from. My ancestors are Native Americans.'

Coco looked at Mack in admiration. He watched the firelight reflect on his umber skin and noticed a sad tinge in his deep dark brown eyes that sparkled like the furthest stars above them. Coco had read all about the Native Americans and how they were a proud and noble race. He had never thought for one moment he would meet one face to face, he was so awestruck by Mack at that moment he could not speak. Then he chuckled to himself as he thought about how the Ringmaster had announced that Mack had charmed his mermaid wife Michelle out of the sea.

Mack picked up his guitar again and started to sing. He sang a happy song and Coco smiled when he finished.

Coco asked him, 'you know how you told me when we first met that you had really good hearing and that you could hear the swords pass each other in the air when you were juggling them?'

'Yes,' said Mack, 'but as I also said, a lot of its practice. There are no short cuts with swordsmanship. Saying that, you're doing really well with your learning, Coco.'

'Thanks, Mack. I wanted to say that I also have keen hearing, it's one of the strange talents; also, my eyesight's also really sharp, like I can zoom in on things in a way.' Then Coco laughed. 'I still wouldn't like to do sword juggling blindfolded, but I am enjoying all the sword fighting lessons.'

Coco jumped up and, picking up a stick, started to show Mack some new moves he had been practicing.

Mack looked up and smiled. 'You're welcome, Coco. I've noticed that, like me, you can fight equally with both hands.'

Coco jabbed the stick at an imaginary opponent and then sat down and tossed the stick into the small fire. He asked Mack, 'So if you are American, how come you're here in England?'

Mack kicked his boots off and settled back down, leaning on his bag for support, before replying. 'Well, it wasn't long after I married Michelle. I'd been married before, but I left everything after my first marriage ended so was penniless. Michelle and I fell in love at first sight, being a mermaid she had no money either but as you can see, she's a bit of a rarity. We made a plan to save up and settle down somewhere. At first, we hooked up with a travelling show and then our paths crossed with this circus who offered us a better deal and so we joined. We've been travelling a few years and have more than enough saved now, but I kind of like travelling around. I really want an adventure; you'll probably laugh at me now, Coco, but I wish I could travel back in time and be a real pirate.'

Coco's eyes widened, he felt the blood course through his body, and a small idea started to form in his brain.

'I think that's a great idea, Mack. You, Eric and I would make the best pirates, and Eric has already managed to make a robot travel back a short way in time. Why, I bet if he had the money and the resources, he could do it. We could go back in time and fight real pirates, what an adventure, Mack!' Coco smiled and felt he had some purpose now. The pair spent the whole night talking, making plans and practicing pirate talk. Both of them realised that they had another strange similarity in the fact that they needed little sleep.

The morning was upon them, the circus train arrived and with it the animals and circus tent.

Mack had arranged that they could stay in that spot for up for a week before everything needed to be packed up again before setting off for the next show ground.

The tent canvas was massive and a hard task to take down and put up again, plus there were all the large poles to move and the rigging. The elephants helped to move things, pulling the ropes and dragging the heavy loads.

Now the train had arrived, Coco appeared to have a million jobs to do and was kept busy, but still found some quiet time to find his friend Eric and tell him of Mack's idea.

Coco found Eric working on a new electrical invention, a small robot that would fly around the circus tent. It used clockwork and steam and mirrors and crystals and large batteries to work. Eric listened as Coco excitedly talked.

Eric smiled and said, 'yes, oh yes, Coco, this is possible, but we will need huge resources and a settled place. The three of us will make plans. For now, Coco, work on your act as, if you can persuade the Ring Master to let you do it, this will bring in a lot of money.'

It was a Friday, once a week the Ring Master would ask to see how Coco was getting on with his act. Each time he thought it was good enough, the Ringmaster would watch and then say, 'No, not ready.' This had been going on now for two months. Coco was getting a dab hand at packing up the boxes of costumes and carefully wrapping the plumes of feathers.

Whenever they got to a new showground and everything was nearly set up, Coco and some of the other boys were put in charge of taking flyers around and offering free tickets to the shop owners who displayed a poster in their windows.

It was on this day that Coco met a very interesting person who was to become an important part of his life. He was the owner of a special shop.

It was called Tippy Toys and Magic Shop.

Coco went in to give them a poster and was impressed by the collection of amazing toys. There were wind up ones and ones that balanced on wires stretched across the ceiling of the shop.

There were colourful posters on the walls about past magic shows.

The shopkeeper was a tall, thin man with grey thinning hair and a waxed moustache.

When he saw Coco come in, he took off his bowler hat and a white bird flew from it.

'Welcome, welcome,' he said.

'Hello, Sir, please could you put up this poster?' Coco asked, holding one out for him to see.

The shopkeeper smiled a wonderful warm smile and held out his hand to take the poster, 'But of course, I wouldn't miss it for the world. The circus is the greatest show on earth.'

He took the poster and handed Coco a daisy.

Coco laughed and looked at the posters on the wall. He noticed that in all of them there appeared a man who looked very much like the shopkeeper. The title beneath his image said,' Mesmer the Amazing Mind Reader.'

'Oh, so,' said Coco thoughtfully, 'you were a mind reader.'

'Yes, lad, that's right,' the shopkeeper said. 'I was Mesmer, the most amazing mind reader.' He took off his hat and bowed. 'Lend me your hand and I'll read your mind.'

'Really?' Coco said, not sure whether or not to give his hand.

'Yes really,' he said, slightly impatient as he held his gloved hand out to Coco.

Coco placed his hand on the shopkeeper's who said, 'arrh, I can see you have had a charmed life. Do you own any metal objects?'

Coco took off the St Christopher around his neck and offered it to him to study.

The shopkeeper placed it on a red velvet cushion and then carefully took off his gloves, held it hard and then closed his eyes tight.

Coco watched in wonder as the shopkeeper seemed to go into a sort of trance.

Finally, he said, 'Boy, you have run away from a religious upbringing, and you have special skills.'

Coco thought he probably guessed that. It was clear he was part of the circus as he was handing out the leaflets. Plus, it was kind of obvious he had a religious upbringing as he wearing the necklace of a saint. Also, as he was in the circus, the chances were that he had run away to join it.

'Hum,' said Coco, not impressed.

'You were born at sea and were given a gift,' he continued.

Coco drew in his breath sharply. 'Yes I was; how did you know that?'

The shopkeeper held his finger to his lips and closed his eyes tight again in concentration.

'I can see you were brought up surrounded by nature but then forced to go and live in a strange place and escaped from a great height.'

'Hum,' said Coco, waiting for more.

'The woman who gave you your name, loved to read children's stories. She was brave and resilient; she taught your life skills. She's dead.'

Coco stood in awe of the shopkeeper.

'Oh I'm sorry,' he said, passing back the necklace as he did not want to look further into it.

'How did you do that?' Coco demanded to know.

'I'm not quite sure that you understand; you're only young.'

Coco was not put off by this rebuff, so he said, 'I am cleverer than you think. The lady who you referred to, who bought me up, lived in an old monastery that was full of books that the monks had. She has gifted the island and the buildings and books. I spent many evenings reading them. I read about Leonardo and Amadeus and all the Greek classics.'

'Ok simmer down,' the shopkeeper said. 'I will do my best to explain it to you. In all those great books you read, have you come across a phonograph machine?'

Coco shook his head, so the shopkeeper continued. 'Well, this machine records sound on a wax cylinder. The sound is spoken into a trumpet-like device that is connected to the machine and then this is vibrated through a small needle that scratches the sound into the wax cylinder as it turns.

'The sound can then be played back, and you can hear it. It's an ingenious invention; we are living in an amazing period in history. Why almost anything is possible.

'So you see, a bit like the phonograph, if people wear metal objects for a long time, especially if they sleep in them, then somehow the things about them, their experiences, their ambitions and even basic traits about the personality somehow affects the metal at a sub-atomic level. These things, like they have become scarred into it somehow, and me holding the object and concentrating on it, somehow forms a connection and helps me to read them.'

'Wow,' said Coco. 'That's amazing. How old were you when you discovered this gift?'

'I was young as you were, I ran away to the circus just as you did, I and became a magician. At the start it was amazing; I would bend metal with thought and also could tell exact detail about a person from holding a metal object.

'I also helped police to solve crimes that had been committed with a metal object such as a knife.'

Coco interrupted, 'Oh well, hang on; I thought that the metal object needed to be in contact for a long while to make a recording.'

'Yes, clever lad, well spotted, this is true unless there is something extreme that touches the metal, such as violence.

'But the police did not convict anyone just on what I said; no, they used modern techniques like fingerprinting.'

Coco was puzzled, 'So you were in the circus. Why did you give it up?'

'They're not all good people, you know,' the shopkeeper said solemnly.

Coco looked surprised.

The shopkeeper continued, 'some circus people are great, and many are ok, but a few have a dark streak of evil running through them. I never trusted the clowns myself, the ones who never took their makeup off. I noticed that they also steered clear of me and made sure never to let me touch any metal they held, even the knives and forks they ate with they kept on their person the whole time.

'I think in the end, their paranoia spread around the circus and other performers started to become wary of me. They made up stories to get rid of me, so as I could tell what they were planning, I left.

'I also didn't like the way they treated the animals. The dogs were fine, but the circus I was in had tigers that they kept cooped up in small cages and made them jump through rings of fire. I just felt it was sad and mean.'

Coco nodded. 'My circus just has elephants, they are worked really hard and made to do tricks. I have seen the trainer prick them really hard with a sharp spike on his stick. I feel they're sad. It's a shame as they are such beautiful and intelligent animals.'

There was a silent pause in the conversation in which they both were lost in their own thoughts about the animals, which was broken by Coco asking, 'So do you like it here, staying in one spot, I mean?'

The shopkeeper looked sad and said, 'I don't really miss the circus that much and certainly not most of the performers, but I do miss the travelling around. It's no fun, though, travelling around on your own and I've been a single man since I settled here.'

Coco smiled. 'Will you come to the circus tonight? I'll be on the door; I have an act I'm working on but haven't finished learning it yet.'

'Yes I'll come, and if you like, afterwards I can watch your act and give you a few pointers.'

'Oh that would be great, thank you, sir.'

As Coco went to the door, the shopkeeper said, 'by the way my name's Greg, that's what my friends call me.'

Coco smiled and waved. 'Thank you, Greg, see you later!'

Coco hurried back and arrived and was given some more jobs to do before the evening and the performance began.

When it was time for the show to start, Coco looked around for Greg and spied him on a front row seat on the other side of the main ring.

He went over and sat next to him, and the pair of them shared popcorn while they watched the show.

It was a splendid show and after it finished they waited for everyone to leave. After about ten minutes, there was no one left, and the tent had an eerie silence to it.

Coco stood on one of the elephants stands, took out a long thin square shaped tube, held it up and then started to squeeze through it.

It was not long before he was out the other side.

At first, Greg was speechless then he said, 'in all my life I have never seen an act like that! That's a special skill, is there anything else you can do, lad?'

Coco beamed and excitedly said, 'Yes, a couple of things. When I first escaped from the orphanage, I was very scared, I had run away and was hiding in a shop doorway when I heard my name being called. I looked around the doorway where I was sheltering from the wind and saw people coming along the street looking for me. I was terrified as I'd made up my mind never to go back to the orphanage, but there was nowhere to hide, so I just stood still and to my amazement they didn't see me.

'They must have looked right at me and, as I said, there was nowhere to hide and I couldn't have outrun them, but then they passed and appeared to look straight through me.

'It was then I looked at my reflection in the shop window. I saw that I'd disappeared, blended into the wall of the shop.

'Also, when I'm scared or angry, this inky liquid forms out of my fingers. Plus, I can also swim really well and fast. I rescued Mary, the lady who brought me up, after she jumped into the sea, by swimming and dragging her backwards in a storm, even with a broken arm.'

'Well now, that's a brave thing to do. I know I can trust you, boy, as I felt it when I touched the metal medallion of St Christopher.'

'Thanks,' said Coco. 'I don't have many friends. There's Mack and his wife who is a real mermaid, and there's Eric, who I will introduce you to. His act wasn't on tonight, as he had to go out of town, but he should be back by now.'

'I would love to meet him. But first, to your act. It's mighty impressive, but what you're lacking is a bit of showmanship.'

'Showmanship?' Coco questioned.

'Yes, you need to build the suspense. Is there a pretty girl you can have as you assistant?'

'Oh there's loads of pretty girls here, Megan's probably the prettiest,' Coco gushed.

'Well pick one and get them to wear something skimpy, like stockings and a corset, feathers in their hair.

'Get the girl to hold up your tube like this and walk around the ring showing everybody that there is nothing inside it.

'Here let me show you.' Coco watched as Greg walked as girl-like as he could. He walked around the room, holding the tube up, stopping now and then and showing it to a pretend member of the audience, for their examination.

'Yes, but what am I supposed to be doing while this all goes on?'

'Misdirection,' said Greg. 'First you stand with your arms in the air, and everyone looks at you, then when the pretty girl enters, you point with both arms to her, and then with your arms out wide you continue to point to her, all eyes will follow the girl. Do you have a costume?'

'Oh yes, there making me one that looks like an octopus,' Coco laughed. 'I won't be able to fit into the space with it on, though; it's got eight huge legs/arms stuck on to it!'

Greg looked thoughtful. 'So if I were you, I would walk around the ring once in it, waving, just to keep the Ringmaster happy. Then wear a long cloak, as all eyes are on the girl, wrap the cloak around you and slip out of the costume, wear a black leotard and black tights underneath it, you know like the acrobats do.'

'Ok,' said Coco. 'That's great advice, thanks.'

Greg continued, 'Also when you've finished your act, stand up and raise your arms over your head and turn around. Get the girl to point to you. Then hand her the tube and let her walk again with it around the ring, showing everyone, here is where you take your bow.'

'Thank you, that's great, Greg, I feel much better about it all.'

Greg smiled. 'You're welcome. Follow these simple stages and it will make it into more of an act rather than just a freak side show.'

'Would you like to meet Eric now?' Coco asked.

'I would indeed, lead on.' Greg followed Coco across the ring and out of the tent flaps at the end. It was a short walk over to Eric's tent. From the outside, they could see sparks flying.

'Eric's an inventor as well,' Coco said proudly.

Greg waited politely behind Coco as he called out to his friend.

Eric came out and invited them in.

Coco had already told Eric about Greg, and the two of them started talking at once about machinery and cogs and clockwork and the like.

Greg opened his bag and put down on the small wooden table a beautiful ballerina toy. It had pale skin, yellow hair and blue eyes and was dressed in a pink dress tutu with pink ballet shoes fashioned, so the dancer stood on tiptoes.

The two young men were engaged in deep discussions about machinery and building robots. Coco watched in fascination, he knew this was the start of a new friendship and was glad of it. Mack came in, and the conversation got on to the possibility of travelling back in time and fighting real pirates. Greg said he would love that; he told them he had no family to speak of and already had amassed quite a small fortune, so they made a pact then and there, that when the time was right, they would send for Greg so he could be a part of it. Now there were four crew members and one mermaid for the time travelling pirate ship!

Chapter 4

(4th Arm).

The Act, First Time

After the performance tips that Greg had given Coco on his circus act, he was at last beginning to feel a lot more confident about performing it in front of the Ringmaster. Over the next few days, he put in some more practice and had a dress rehearsal in his Octopus costume. Friday came around again, and Coco stood in front of the entire circus group in full costume as the Ringmaster watched. Everyone cheered after he finished his act and Coco took a bow. Mack rushed over and patted him on the back. The Ringmaster seemed pleased and approved the act on the spot. He told Coco that it would be included in the very next show.

On the day of his first show, Coco felt that, even with all the long preparation and extensive rehearsals, the thought of performing his act live in front of the crowds made him feel more and more anxious the nearer the hour came. The Ringmaster had new posters printed, proclaiming Coco 'The Octopus Boy,' as the star attraction and Coco began to feel under some strain with the added extra pressure.

Coco's friends were excited for him and made a big fuss that day. Eric teased him slightly about the posters but in a nice way. The pair had also been working on a new act for Eric's show and that morning Coco had watched from the ringside excitedly as Eric stood out into the centre to perform his electrical show. Coco smiled in wonder as the robot disappeared and he dreamt of the time travelling pirate adventures that they would all have together one day.

Coco was at last beginning to feel safe and happy in his new life and valued Eric and Mack's friendship and was so glad that he had found them.

The circus tent had been raised, and everything was in place for the show to start. This was the first performance of the week at the rural village of Church Crookham, a small hamlet in Hampshire. Throngs of excited folk, who had travelled from miles around, were milling about the show ground, looking at the various colourful sideshows and picking their way down towards the main tent.

Everyone had on their finest clothes. The rosy-cheeked field workers wore straw hats with bright ribbons tied around the brims and the young village girls had on their crisp white dresses and had poppies and daisies picked from the fields strewn in their long hair. There was a happy noise of chatter and excited squeals from the youngsters. The smell of hot fatty food hung in the air and homemade Scrumpy cider was being shared liberally by the locals.

As circus shows went, this was small and one in which the troupe hardly cut a profit. The Ringmaster still kept the stop in this village out of tradition more than profit. Also, it was rumoured that he had fathered several children in this village, so it gave him a chance to visit his offspring and their mothers. Plus, it was a good place to stop half way between the two larger shows of Southampton and London.

The small red brick houses which lined the twisty roads of the picturesque village were mostly occupied by field workers; apple and hop pickers, seasonal at that. But nicer cheerier folk you could not hope to meet and they always welcomed entertainment and were free in return with their own hospitality and homemade brew.

Eric also had a new lady friend who he had been quite struck by. She was living in the nearby tavern working as a bar wench. Coco teased Eric as he watched him take extra care with his costume and make-up that night, making a point of noting the amount of extra time Eric took as he ironed his shirt and blacked his boots.

Mack was making some last minute preparations to a new sword juggling segment of his show. A group of small children were stood at a distance, pointing in wonder at him, as Mack threw the blades high into the air and caught them in his teeth. He took the blades out of his mouth and bowed and smiled at the children who scurried away, chuckling. As Mack peered out into the main arena, he could see the audience jostling to get the best seats. He noted that for a supposedly small show in a small village, this night it had appeared that just about every seat had been taken. They had all come to see the incredible new act of 'Octopus Boy,' as promised by the posters and the crowd buzzed with excitement.

All the performers in the circus traditionally had to double as ticket sales people or ushers before the show started, so Mack made his way over to the entrance to do his bit, selling programs and signing a few for the adoring local village women who swooned and giggled when he handed them back. Outside, some of the circus freaks were performing small acts to get the people drawn into the main tent. The bearded lady was stroking her long beard; the tattooed lady was completely naked apart from a few carefully placed clam shells and the Siamese twins performed yoga moves together on a high plinth.

Michelle the mermaid was swimming around in her tank near the entrance and waving at the good folk as they came in.

Mack looked at the large clock over the band stage area. It was nearly 6 pm and most people were already settled in their seats. Mack put down the programmes, took up his swords and started to perform a dazzling show of swordsmanship while the excited village folk looked on, causing some of the young women to shout out his name in admiration. At 6 pm on the dot the band, who had been warming up their instruments, struck up a song and the pink and blue circus spotlights danced around the tent like a magical promise.

Just outside the tent, Coco was selling portions of cold custard from a small candy striped stand. As he spooned small amounts into decorated paper cups, he thought about his upcoming performance as Octopus Boy and his heart began to race. Already he could hear the band starting up and playing its first song. Umpa, umpa. He could also hear the elephants roar at the back of the tent, waiting to go into the ring and the squealing ropes being pulled through the pulleys as the tightrope cables were secured. All of a sudden Coco felt it all melded into one loud noise which was magnified by the screams of excited children to a deafening level. He looked around for his friends as the tent and lights spun in a hypnotic way in front of him.

Coco began to feel sick and wobbly. His mouth had a salty bile taste to it, and he began to break out in a panic sweat. His head started to pound, and he had trouble breathing. He noticed the faces in the crowd appeared to lurch in front of him. Then, without further warning, he keeled over, his whole body sweating and trembling. He felt like his bones were made from jelly. A thick black liquid oozed from his fingertips. This was the last thing he saw before all his senses left him and he blacked out.

Moments later, still feeling short of breath, he suddenly shot up and started gasping for air. All the circus lights were still spinning in front of him. A small crowd of people were circled about him when Eric broke, though. 'Stand back!' he shouted. 'Give him some air! Are you all right, Coco?' he asked breathlessly.

Coco sat up straighter and supported the weight of his body onto his arms. He gazed around him at the onlookers' faces. He managed to push the words out in a shallow sentence, 'I'm fine.'

Eric looked relieved as he heard the Ringmaster shouting at the crowd. 'Ok, there's nothing to see here!' The Ringmaster's face appeared between the onlookers; he seemed flustered and sweaty as he ran from behind, still hurriedly dressing himself for the start of the performance. His fine red coat had only one arm in it, and his white shirt collar was hanging on by one button. 'Move along!' he shouted louder at the now gaping audience, flapping his arms in an attempt to herd the people in the direction of the main tent. Finally, they started to drift away with the flapping Ringmaster at their backs. After a short distance, he jogged back, his belly wobbling with his unexpected run and returned to gaze down at Coco. Then, giving a worried glance towards Eric, asked, 'Will the boy be able to go on tonight?'

Eric silently looked at Coco, whose complexion was as white as a sheet.

'Oh I'm sure I'll be fine,' Coco said in a hesitant voice, not waiting for Eric's opinion.

Eric said, 'I'll make him a hot cup of sweet tea. That will perk him up.'

The Ringmaster nodded in approval while straightening his red jacket and finishing the buttoning on his white collar.

'Very well,' he said. 'I'll bump the Octopus Boy act up to the very end of the show, to give him a chance to recover.'

Eric helped Coco into the changing area at the back of the tent. He made him the tea and handed it to him. 'You all right now, lad?'

Just then Mack came charging through to the tent and knelt down beside Coco. 'I just heard,' he said. He had a worried look on his face. 'Are you all right, my friend?'

Coco, a little embarrassed by the attention, said, 'I'm fine, thank you both, please don't fuss.'

Coco sipped the tea; there was far too much sugar in it, but he drank it down and managed a smile at the men. 'I'm fine, promise,' he said again.

Mack rested his hand on Coco's shoulder and said, 'Lad, just concentrate on doing your act. I've seen you do it a few times now. I think the crowd will be amazed, they won't have seen anything like that before. I bet they will clap and even cheer. You'll be a hit; I'm sure of it. Now, if you've finished your tea, come out with me and watch my act.'

Mack helped Coco to his feet, and Eric carried Coco's Octopus costume for him. Coco stood at the ringside watching the acts as they took place. Eric and Mack stood next to him. After a while, Mack said, 'well then, Coco, it's time for me to go on. Do you think you will be ok now?'

Coco rolled his eyes to the top of his head in frustration.

Mack continued to make a fuss and said, 'take your time, take a breath and get some water if you need some and compose yourself.'

Coco stood up as tall as he could. 'I'm fine now,' he said rather abruptly. 'It must just have been a touch of nerves. I mean, I was a bit scared. I thought about all those children at the orphanage who teased me, and now I am billed as top freak! I mean, that's a bit much at my age to take on board, plus when I get scared or upset, this black ink substance flows out of my fingernails.' Coco held his hands up for them to see.

'Don't worry about that, Coco,' said Eric reassuringly, taking out his handkerchief, spitting on it and wiping the inky substance away while saying, 'you should have seen me the first time I took the stage. I was terrified! I stumbled over my words and then started to talk in French, and I felt as if I'd pass out under the glare of the lights.'

Coco smiled, and they stood together and watched Mack's act silently. It was amazing as always. Mack climbed up to the tightrope and then, blindfolded, walked out onto it. He held juggling batons above his head and then he took matches out of his pocket and struck them to light the batons. He walked along the rope, juggling the flaming batons high into the air and catching each of them. Then, taking a bow, he walked across to the other side of the rope and handed the batons to a beautiful lady, collected his swords and ran back along the tightrope, juggling the swords as he went. Coco held his breath, it did not matter to him, however, many times he saw Mack's act, he was always amazed by it and his skill. After Mack's act had finished, Eric said, 'look, chap, I have to go on now, I can hear the Ringmaster announcing my act. Are you going to be all right?'

Coco answered Eric in French, 'Oui, Oui,' (yes, yes).

And the pair laughed.

Coco felt much better as he started to climb into his octopus suit.

He heard the drums, tut, tut, then a drum roll. And then a spotlight. He watched as his friend Eric jumped into the light in the ring.

Eric held his hands out wide. He was wearing a long black cloak which had a dark blue silk lining. He was holding his top hat in his right hand. The audience cheered as he bowed and then from behind him; much slower, rolled his Robot.

The crowd gasped, and little children pointed at the robot in a questioning manner.

Eric announced, in a long drawn out serious tone, 'Ladies and gentlemen; tonight you will be witness to one of the greatest mystery's known to modern man.' There was a pause for effect and a small drum roll. Eric spread his arms wide so that the light caught the blue silk of his lining and small sparks appeared around him as he shouted the word, 'transportation!'

Everyone clapped as the drum roll started up again and then stopped with a crash of a cymbal.

Eric took a bow again, undid his cape and placed it on a chair along with his top hat.

Then he undid his cufflinks and placed them in his pocket and rolled up the sleeves on his pinstriped shirt.

Every gesture that he made was over exaggerated, and the crowd watched his every move in silence.

Then the lights dimmed, and the spotlights flew around the circus top, then stopped to light up the robot. Everyone one was amazed as the panel on top of the robot's head started to light up, and small green lights flashed and flickered into life. Then large electric sparks flew around the robot, and it hovered slightly off the floor. The crowd gasped.

There was one more drum roll as the tension mounted. Eric placed a cloak over his robot and then, with a flick of his wrist he removed it and it was gone. Everyone gasped.

The spotlights that had been roaming around the tent stopped at the far end and, much to the audience's surprise, focused on the robot.

Everyone clapped and Eric took several bows.

Next the Ringmaster brought on the elephants and Coco, as always, watched spellbound as the elephants went through their act, balancing on their hind legs while their front two were on large balls.

Afterwards, they waved flags as they marched around the circus ring. All the children waved their flags back at them. They were huge elephants, which must have seen like giants to the small children. The elephants did look splendid that day they had large red white and blue plumes in gold crowns on their heads. Such beautiful and majestic animals, Coco thought.

Next a brand new act of acrobats came on. They sported long black plaits of hair. Coco had heard that they had come from Budapest. They wore flared green baggy trousers, and bronze flecked tops. Coco was mesmerized.

The Budapest acrobats must have been practicing since childhood; they were incredible. The Ringmaster had told Coco that they used to be top billing in their last show, but in this show Coco's new act, Octopus Boy, was to be the top spot and that he should be proud of that. After the act had finished, the trapeze artists swung above his head. Megan was wearing a beautiful purple jewelled tutu that evening, with sapphire feathers. She flew through the air between catches, spinning with ease, wowing the audience.

All too soon it was Coco's turn. The drums rolled, the Ringmaster called out his act. 'Ladies and gentlemen, now for the very first time, I present to you our all new star attraction, drum roll please, I present, Octopus Boy!'

The band struck up a jolly song and Michelle the Mermaid made sea noises as Coco walked around the ring, showing off his octopus costume. The children smiled and waved to him while their parents clapped loudly as he walked around. The costume was green and shiny, little sequins sparkled in the circus lights and Coco lifted all the legs in the air as he paraded around the ring. This was easy for him to do as they were tied together with clear thread so that he could wave them all at the same time. His thick curly hair was held up so that the audience could see the squid-like growths on the back of his neck.

The Ringmaster was impressed at how Coco played the crowd. Coco remembered the advice from Greg where he said,' don't do your act at once, there's no use in just doing your act. There is no showmanship in that. And showmanship is king.'

After Coco had walked around the ring, he stood in the middle and held his arms up in the air, so as to show the full extent and colours of his brightly coloured costume. A young girl dressed in the most dazzling sailor costume came in from the side. Her costume was covered in red, white and blue sequins in the pattern of an American flag, with a sequined beret to match. She walked around, showing a thin metal tube to the audience.

Coco pointed to her as she did this and then all eyes fell on the girl.

While she walked slowly around, carefully showing the tube, Coco went to the ringside and slipped out of his octopus costume before returning into the centre of the ring and looking down silently, waiting for the noise in the audience to still and be completely quiet. Then there was a drum roll, and the girl in the sailor costume handed Coco the tube.

Then the drumming stopped, and there was almost total silence. The crowd held their breath.

Coco waved the tube around his head once more before placing it on the elephant stand and slowly started to squash his body through the small gap. Within less than a minute he was through.

Everybody gasped when he appeared from the other side, and they stood up and clapped.

Next, another pretty ringside assistant in a fine boned pink corset with ostrich feathers in her hair walked into the ring carrying a much smaller longer tube. As she carried it, she held it up so all could see down through the thin narrow shape.

The drum rolled again as the pretty assistant laid the tube-shaped box on top of the elephants' stand. Both girls stood back and opened their arms to point to Coco. He waved to everybody then slowly began to squash himself thought the smaller tube.

It was amazing to watch and not humanly possible. Coco, remembering what Greg had said about showmanship, pretended to be stuck in the middle for a bit. Both girls put their hands to their mouths and made over-exaggerated gasps, and the audience held its breath. Coco paused for one moment more, and even the Ringmaster began to think he was stuck. Then Coco did one more push before forcing his way through the tube.

When he arrived on the other side, he jumped up triumphantly, holding his hands wide and spinning around so everyone could see that he was a normal boy again. The two girls clapped, Coco bowed, and all the audience cheered and clapped. Coco felt surprised as while he was performing the act he had not felt nervous at all, he was so pleased that no one laughed or called him a freak.

The Ringmaster ran on and took off his hat to him. Holding his back tall and straight and throwing open his arms, he pointed to Coco and everyone clapped again.

Then Coco took another bow and then another and the noise of the audience erupted into a crescendo as he run out of the circus ring, waving.

The Ringmaster quickly followed him and patted him on the back, said, 'well done, well done! We'll have packed audiences from now on.'

Coco looked at the large smile that the Ringmaster had on his face, and he could almost see money signs flash in the man's eyes.

The band stuck up the farewell music, and all the circus folk and the elephants and white horses with their beautiful plumes balanced on their heads went around the ring once more, and the fat lady sang.

So that was Coco's first show, and he had many more and, true to his word, all the money went towards Eric's experiments. Mack and Michelle also put their money into the pot towards the time travelling equipment. Every evening, after all, the work was done for the day, you could find the small group of Coco, Eric, Mack and Michelle huddled together, talking late into the night, making exciting plans about travelling back in time and fighting real bloodthirsty cutthroat Pirates.

In between the shows Coco wrote long letters to Greg to keep him informed of any developments, so that he would feel part of the group.

Everything went well for Coco, and he settled in with ease to his new life, until, after just two more years, disaster stuck.

In every way, it was an accident. Coco had finished his act for the evening and the knife throwing act was about to go on. However, there was a problem as the lady who performed in the act with her husband had just found out that she was pregnant. She was in floods of tears as she had been arguing with her husband. He had been drinking; she was complaining that it was bad enough that he was risking her life each time that they did the act, but now there was a baby as well to consider.

She was young, pretty lady with fiery red hair and a temperament to match and the shouting match quickly escalated into a screaming as her husband shouted back at her, waving his fists in a threatening manner.

Coco, not sure what to do, called Mack who came over and managed to stand between the knife thrower and his wife. Coco sat on the floor next to the girl, who was now crying so hard he had trouble making out her words between sobs. 'He got me pregnant. I can't believe he's angry, surely in this condition he can see that I can't be the one who has the knives thrown at them, not now, plus he's been drinking. I can smell it. He's an animal, an animal, I tell you and I shan't do his rotten stinking act!' She started to shake, and Coco put an arm around her shoulders in a bid to calm her.

The knife thrower and his wife had been one of the original acts that formed the circus and as such the Ringmaster had cut them some slack out of loyalty. Everyone knew that they argued something terrible as a couple and that she had a quick temper and that he was a drinker. However, with that said, he was the best knife thrower that everyone had ever seen, and he had never missed, although at times the Ringmaster felt that with such an argumentative wife such as that he must have been tempted.

The minutes ticked by and at last Mack managed to calm the knife thrower down enough so that he had stopped shouting. The Ringmaster looked at a loss but then, in a flash of inspiration, volunteered Coco into the act as a standby. Coco was not worried as he had seen for himself that the knife thrower never missed. Mack was not worried also as he helped Coco put on his octopus costume, which he had suggested he wore to make the act a bit more interesting.

Coco felt it was an odd experience have the knives thrown towards him; he knew not to move. He was a bit scared but in his head told himself that this was good pirate training.

The act went off without a hitch; however the next day next day the knife thrower's wife announced to the Ringmaster and everybody that she did not want to do the act again. The Ringmaster called a meeting to see if any of the other pretty girls in the show would stand in for her while she was going through her pregnancy.

Not surprisingly, none of them wanted to do the act. The Ringmaster turned again to Coco, and said, 'do you think you can do it every show, lad? There will be extra money in it for you.'

Coco agreed on the spot as he knew that some extra money would help with buying parts for Eric's experiments.

Sadly, just a few weeks later, there was some complication with the knife thrower's wife's pregnancy, and she miscarried. When the knife thrower heard the news about the dead baby he was upset and drank hard all that day.

Eric spotted it and tried to stop the act going on, but the Ringmaster would have none of it. He said, 'well, we all know he likes to drink, he's often quite drunk while performing the act but he never misses!'

So the scene was set. The drummer hit his drums, Tut tut, tut, then a drum roll.

The spotlight flicked menacingly on the board where Coco was tied and then the knife thrower threw his first blade which narrowly missed Coco's ear. Coco held his breath; the knife thrower did his best to focus; that had been too close for comfort, and he knew it. Steadying himself, he threw his second blade, it hit the top of Coco's octopus costume, shearing the top layer of sequins off. Without pausing, the knife thrower threw his third blade. The audience held their breath and then there was one shrill scream from the knife thrower's wife as she spotted that his hand had slipped, and the blade did not run true. The knife ricocheted with force into Coco, and the audience cried out in shock. The knife had hit Coco's arm badly. Coco screamed as blood gushed out and then he fainted. Mack darted towards the knife thrower, knocking the remaining blades from his hand and wrestling him to the ground. Eric rushed into the ring to the board to untie his friend and carry him to the back of the tent.

The Ringmaster quickly sent the clowns in to do an act and Megan, who had been watching from above, swung down to run over to help.

Coco was carried out and into a side tent and Mack hurriedly rode into the village to fetch a doctor. Megan wrapped pieces of torn sheets around the badly bleeding arm and elevated it, in an attempt to stop the bleeding.

Some time later when Coco came to, the knife thrower, Mack, Eric, Megan, the Ringmaster and a doctor were all stood around him.

The knife thrower started to apologize. He was shaking and visibly upset. Eric was in shock, his face pale white. He could not speak.

It was Mack who spoke first. 'Coco, I have some news for you, I am afraid it's not good news, so you need to prepare yourself.'

Megan rested an arm on Coco's shoulder in a steadying manner and looked into Coco's terrified eyes.

Coco drew a sharp breath and prepared himself as best he could, although he still felt in a bit of a daze.

Mack's deep brown eyes started to fill with tears as he tenderly spoke. 'Coco, I'm afraid the doctor had to remove the lower part of your left arm. '

Coco raised his arm; it was then that he realized that it had been severed just under the elbow, on the left-hand side.

'No!' cried Coco, feeling faint.

The doctor took some painkiller into a syringe and said, 'look; the morphine will help. I'm sorry I could not save your arm. I have to say Megan's quick thinking binding your arm and my surgery saved your life.'

Mack spoke to the doctor. 'We are all grateful to you, Doctor for your skill, thank you.'

Eric could not find the right words to say to comfort Coco so just stood next to him and patted him on his shoulder.

Megan gathered all the bloodstained rags together and quietly carried them out of the tent.

The Ringmaster said, in a blustering voice, 'never mind, you don't need the arm to do your act, you still have your job, boy, could have been worse.'

Mack threw an angry look at the Ringmaster, and Coco tried to be brave, and he bit back the tears and fought with the vomit that was tracking up his throat.

The Ringmaster paid the doctor and then gave a stern look to the knife thrower and told him to wait outside for him.

Eric had slumped back onto the floor again, but Mack was standing next to Coco's bed and glared after the knife thrower, with half a mind to go after him. Coco noticed Mack's unease and grabbed his sleeve so he would stay with him.

The Ringmaster, uneasy at the change in Mack's mood, held his hand up in a steadying gesture and backed out the tent, promising that would be the last they saw of the knife thrower and his wife.

After he had left the tent, Michelle came in, manoeuvring herself over to Coco's bedside in a wheelchair on which she had delicately balanced a tray with some tomato soup and buttered white bread.

Coco caught the scent of warm tomato and felt the vomit hit the top of his throat. He leant over to one side as he could longer stop the sick from emptying from his stomach. Michelle wiped Coco's face with a wet warm flannel and Mack moved the offending soup over to the other side of the tent so that the smell could no longer bother him.

Coco looked around at his friends, his mind racing with the severity of his new situation. Then he closed his eyes and slept a sleep that was mostly induced by the high dosage of morphine and was not restful in the least.

Mack and Eric stayed with Coco that night to keep him company. Later, when he woke, he was in a little pain and groggy. They tried to cheer him up by talking about time travel and fighting real pirates.

Eric tried to make a joke by saying, 'Coco, you look like a real pirate now, Captain Hook!'

Coco tried to smile, and Mack gave Eric a sideways glance and then told them both one of his favourite Greek legend stories about how the Greek hero Perseus rescued Princess Andromeda from a ghastly sea monster. He stood up and made shadow puppets with of his hands on the side of the tent.

And so an uneasy night was spent among the three men, but their bond of friendship was strengthened because of it.

Coco was allowed one week's complete rest, after which the Ringmaster gave him light duties, and he was excused from his Octopus Boy performances for the following six weeks. Coco did his best to remain happy and positive and was pleased to have been granted his first wish of helping feed and care for the circus elephants.

After the six weeks' probationary period had passed, the doctor came to assess Coco's stump. He was shocked to find that a squid-like growth had sprouted out of the wound.   Coco had noticed the growth appearing and realised that it was similar in feel and touch to the tubes on the back of his neck but much thicker and more like an octopus's arm.

It was another two weeks until the doctor came again and this time, he found that the Ringmaster measured Coco's new octopus arm. All three were surprised how much it had grown; it was now two-foot long.

Eric, Mack and all the circus troupe admired Coco's new growth, which seemed to grow a little longer each day that followed until it was over twice the size of his original arm and could extend even further if he willed it.

Coco discovered with delight that his new octopus arm could move and function just as much as his normal arm did, but with additional qualities. Things about it were uniquely special, far superior to his other arm. Each of the suckers was extremely sensitive and seemed able to seek things out and feel and could taste the air and sense all types of things for themselves. It was as if part of his brain had moved into his arm and he felt more alive for it.

 Coco and Mack practiced their swordplay daily, and Coco discovered that with a sword in his new octopus arm, he was a fearsome fighter.

Within just a few days Mack was, for the first time, beaten by Coco. When Eric came in and saw Mack un-armed and backed up against the tent flaps, all three laughed together and slapped each other on the back like chaps do. Mark said that as Coco was now the superior swordsman he should be the captain when they got the ship. Before Coco could protest; Eric seconded it, so that was it. That was how Coco was named the captain in readiness for the time travelling pirate ship.

� ⁁

Chapter 5

(Arm 5).

Coco the Star

Coco and Eric headed over to the Ringmaster's brightly painted caravan to ask him about Coco restarting his act now his arm was better. They both felt confident as the Ringmaster had been true to his word and had given Coco paid employment while his arm healed. Coco, in turn, had enjoyed feeding and looking after the elephants for the past few weeks. However, he was keen to get back to doing the act and thought his new octopus arm would be a good draw for the paying public.

The Ringmaster was still in his pyjamas when Coco and Eric arrived at his caravan. A young local village woman was just letting herself out; she held the door open so that they could enter.

The Ringmaster smiled at them both and ushered them inside before waving goodbye and blowing a kiss to the now giggling woman.

Evidently in a good mood, the Ringmaster happily re-negotiated the return of Coco's act and also promised a pay raise and said that new posters were to be printed, showing his new octopus arm and proclaiming "octopus' boy" king of the show.

Eric had stood silently throughout the whole meeting, but just before Coco agreed to the new terms, he leaned down and whispered into Coco's ear that he should ask for quite a bit more money now that he had his new arm and reminded him of a particular piece of machinery that he needed to buy.

Coco did ask for more money and, to his surprise, the Ringmaster agreed straight away.

The new posters were prepared, and Coco worked on his showmanship. Within a few weeks, his act was the talk of the town, top billing, with people paying extra money to shake his octopus arm and have their photo taken with him.

The weeks passed, and Coco enjoyed his new life at the circus and his popularity with the audience.

Eric now had a large pot of money accumulated to buy more machinery so he could carry out new time travel experiments. Everything was progressing very nicely. His newer inventions were getting more and more experimental and the circus folk that walked past his quarters late at night would stop in wonder as they watched magical flashes of coloured light spark about his tent.

Every evening after dinner, Coco, Eric, Mack and Michelle met to discuss their plans, and their bonds of friendship grew ever stronger with each passing night.

In secret, Coco practiced his camouflage skills. He wanted to master this before he told his friends about it, but also planned that this skill could be worked into his circus act somehow.

He discovered that he did not need to be in a terrified state to be camouflaged, he only had to imagine a scary situation and the camouflage would happen. He practiced daily and within a short space of time he was able to hold the state and walk about freely in the show ground quite unnoticed.

He had chosen to introduce the idea of the camouflage to the Ringmaster by walking into his caravan undetected and then re-emerging and then announcing his ideas. Coco chuckled to himself with delight when he thought about how shocked the Ringmaster would be when he popped out of the woodwork in front of him.

The day came when Coco felt he had mastered the camouflage well enough to show the Ringmaster. He had prepared a little speech about how the camouflage could be used in the act as he walked over towards the caravan. When he got there, he waited in his camouflage state until someone opened the door. As it happened, he did not have to wait long, as a familiar person visited that day, someone marched straight up to the door and knocked hard on it.

It was the knife thrower. Coco was more than a little surprised to see the visitor as the knife thrower had been sent away by the Ringmaster the night of Coco's accident and was under strict instructions never to return.

Coco moved as close as he could next to him so he could follow him through the caravan door. The Ringmaster swung open the door and welcomed the knife thrower in. Once inside Coco was again surprised to see that there was another man visiting, the doctor who had saved his life that night. He was already sitting at the table and shot an edgy look at the knife thrower.

Coco stood with his back pushed against the caravan wall, as close as possible to the table where he could observe the three men who had immediately started a heated discussion. The Ringmaster had a plan, it seemed, a deep and dark plan and he needed both the knife thrower and the doctor's involvement to bring it to fruition.

The Ringmaster raised his voice and banged his fist on the small table in an attempt to bring the meeting to order. 'So, as I said before at our previous meeting, Coco has brought a lot of money and notoriety to the circus with his octopus' arm.'

When Coco heard this, he sighed with relief and was about to reveal himself when the doctor said, 'In my medical opinion, I think that there's a good chance that if we remove his other arm and both legs, then more octopus' tentacles will grow.'

Coco gasped so loudly that, for a moment, he was worried he might be detected. He could not believe what he had just heard. He held his breath and sweat formed over his skin; his heart was pounding so loudly that he was worried that he might be heard.

He had no need to think about being scared now to be camouflaged, at that moment he felt terrified beyond words.

The knife thrower chipped in, 'I'm happy to cut them off for a price.'

'Oh, don't worry, you will be amply paid, it's just how to do it, that's all,' the Ringmaster said, whilst dabbing his brow with the end of his neckerchief scarf.

'I think we should kidnap him, then I can slice his limbs off,' the knife thrower said with a thick smile, banging an open blade down on the table.

The doctor grimaced and said, 'Yes, you'd have to give him a shot of something to knock him out stone cold, but I can supply you with that and then rendezvous with you after the deed is done and sew him back up.'

The Ringmaster suddenly stood up, shuddering, feeling nervous as if someone was watching. He stared out of the small window for a whole minute in silence before he sat down to reveal the last part in the dastardly plan. 'I'll raise the alarm when you two have finished; I'll get his unwitting friends, Eric and Mack, to come and help search for him.

'His friends are loyal and will come help look with me; I'll tell them that I had a tip off, and then we'll stumble across Coco and bring him back to the circus and care for him.

'The boy will be so happy to be rescued and grateful to be back with his friends that when he fully recovers, he will do his act again.'

All three men laughed and congratulated themselves on their good plan and how rich they were all going to be.

Coco felt his body sway; he thought he was going to pass out any second. The small caravan was uncomfortably hot, and he felt unstable but did not want to risk sitting down.

Luckily for Coco, the meeting ended at that point, and the knife thrower stood up, placed his cloth cap back on his head and made for the door. As he did so, his arm brushed Coco's body, and the camouflage pattern shimmered.

The knife thrower stopped for a moment and stared at the wall where Coco was standing almost mesmerized. He reached into his pocket to feel his bottle of gin and gained comfort by it. Then, tapping his pocket, he shook his head and walked out the caravan, believing that what he had seen was down to the large amount of alcohol he had been drinking recently.

Coco, who had been holding his breath the whole time the knife thrower was staring in his direction, was on the verge of passing out. He let out a huge sigh and closely followed the knife thrower out of the door.

Once out of the caravan he ran over towards the circus tents to find his friends and tell them of the Ringmaster's shocking plan.

He found them in Eric's tent, watching a demonstration of Eric's new machine. Greg had come on a surprise visit to catch up on developments and to bring some pirate weapons that he had been working on.

Coco, now in the safe company of his friends, un-camouflaged as he burst in through the tent flaps. He stood in the middle of them, shaking and dripping with sweet.

Michelle shouted out to him in shock. 'Coco, what's up? You look like you've seen a ghost!'

Coco desperately tried to form the words in his mind. Mack looked concerned; he put down his sword and walked towards him, holding out a hand to steady the boy. 'What is it, Coco?' he asked, looking anxious, then walked towards the tent flaps and peered out across the circus ground to see if anything had been chasing Coco.

Coco steadied his nerves and, taking a sharp breath, told them all about his camouflaging and how he had snuck into the caravan; who had been there and what the Ringmaster had planned.

Michelle was horrified and wanted to call the police. Mack was angry and wanted to go over to the Ringmaster's caravan and cut his arms and legs off for him. Eric and Greg had to hold Mack down from rushing out and doing this.

Coco finally put an end to the mayhem by saying, 'look, I think it's clear that I can't stay here anymore. I'd be constantly looking over my shoulder. I need to leave the circus today.'

Mack agreed, and Eric made a plan quickly in his head. 'I'm nearly there with the time travel,' he said. 'I think it's time to start to set our plan into action. I propose that Coco and I head off towards Cornwall and try and set up a base camp.

'Mack and Michelle, if you can, stay in the circus for the time being until we are settled and give everyone false information as to where we are heading. And Greg, if you could, take all the equipment back to your shop for now and then forward it to us when I wire you the address. Then if you could make a start at putting your affairs in order and join us down in Cornwall as soon as you can.

Everyone agreed, even although it had been a terrible thing to have heard what the Ringmaster had been planning, Coco began to feel happy and excited that the pirate adventure was about to begin.

Coco and Eric just packed one small bag each to take with them as Michelle said she would look after their other things. She made them a cheese and pickle sandwich each and packed a bottle of homemade cider. Coco carefully packed Mary's journal and one change of clothes into a small canvas rucksack and Eric took his small tool pouch and one change of clothes and added it to his bag. They grabbed the little basket of food from Michelle and, with tears in their eyes, the pair shot from under the tent flaps and started to run toward the train tracks. As luck would have it, a freight train was moving slowly along the track. Eric tossed the bags and the basket onto the open carriage and jumped up in one bound, leaning back and holding his hand out to Coco. Coco ran as fast as he could and, grasping Eric's hand, pulled himself up. Mack, who had followed them to the track, paced along beside the train with ease and shouted, 'good luck, my friends, tell us when you've got settled and are ready, and Michelle and I will follow you down, Captain Coco!'

Coco shouted back, 'I will, my dear friend, we shall meet again soon and be pirates on the sea, Pirate Mack.'

'Arhhh!' shouted Mack, waving his sword in the air as a kind of salute.

Just then the train started to gain speed and lurched away. Mack stopped running and waved frantically to Coco and Eric, who were now grinning from ear to ear with the excitement of it all.

'That was amazing,' Coco said as he fell on the floor of the train carriage next to Eric.

'Have you never jumped a train before?' Eric asked him.

'No never,' Coco laughed.

'Well, there's a first time for everything.'

They sat in silent for a while, listening as the train rattled along the tracks and the wind rushed past them. Coco felt so alive at that moment he could feel the blood pump through his body, he could feel the tubes on the back of his neck tingle with excitement and the suckers on his octopus arm, move about if as tasting the excitement in the air.

Coco grinned. 'There's so much I need to learn, this feels like an adventure.'

'It is an adventure,' Eric said, adding, 'I just hope all our equipment gets to Cornwall safely.'

Coco looked thoughtful. 'Why did you choose Cornwall, Eric?'

'I chose it because my parents have had a holiday home there since I was a child. They live abroad now and left it for me to use, so we can live there for free. I love the area and know it well. The weather is mild in winter, and the docks are deep enough for large ships, and there are shipbuilders in the neighbourhood we can employ.'

Coco felt that Cornwall sounded a good choice and asked, 'do we have enough money to complete the project?'

'Not nearly enough,' said Eric, shaking his head sadly. 'We need to find some backers when we get there and also need to find a safe way to recruit pirates and somewhere that we can train in sword fighting as well as sailing a ship so they can go with us.'

Coco looked worried. 'How will we do that?'

'Well, it won't happen overnight. I can't see the project being complete for at least two years.'

Coco looked a bit sad; he wanted the time travelling adventure to start at once.

Eric noted Coco's disappointment and said, 'I know two years seems a long time to wait, but we'll have a whole ship to build. Anyhow, this will give you time to train with a sword. Sword skills are vital for pirates.'

'I'm already better than you and Mack put together!' Coco said jokingly.

'That you are, Coco, that's why we named you captain. Well, I certainly need the two years to have time to be able to learn to navigate, although you and Mack can already do that and we have Michelle the mermaid who can do navigation naturally, plus we shall also take navigation equipment. I think that I should learn just to be on the safe side.'

Coco smiled and nodded.

The train journey was exciting, and when the train squealed to a halt, they got off at the next station and bought two single tickets to Cornwall. On the way down the pair talked about their plans.

Eric spent some time looking out of the window at the changing countryside and sorting out the plans in his head. Then, wanting to share his thoughts, he turned his gaze to Coco and said, 'We need to set up camp, as it were, and go and mingle with the village folk and try and suss out useful and helpful people as we go. I think it would be best that you keep your octopus arm bound up in a sling, so it appears you've broken it or something.'

Coco nodded and took out his spare shirt. Between them, they made attempts to make a sling out of it and hide the octopus arm.

It was a pleasant journey, and when Coco got his first glimpse of Cornwall from the train window, he was awestruck. The sea was a pure crystal blue, and there were pretty boats bobbing on it. The houses were small and painted bright colours. There was a hilly cliff face, and Coco could see that there were many small shops and pubs. After the train screeched to a halt, they alighted and were met by the wonderful smell of warm Cornish pasties which drifted up as welcome from the station café.

Falmouth, a small coastal town situated on the most south-west tip of England, is a picturesque fishing village. Because of its location and the fact that the weather is so much nicer than the rest of England, the area attracted a huge colony of artists to set up their studio there. It was not long after they had settled into Eric's family house that they met their most useful contact who was one such artist, a colourful character called Morris.

It was Eric who initially struck up a conversation with Morris in a small art gallery on the seafront. Morris's paintings were on display, and Eric was admiring one of the pirates fighting when Morris came over to explain it was one of his. Eric asked a lot of questions about nautical history and the pair got into a long decision which spilled over into a succession of pubs.

Morris, a rich artist in his mid-fifties, had everything money could buy and was well travelled, but his life had lost its sparkle some time earlier. Whether it was the fact that Morris was such a nice chap or the fact that Eric had had a lot of beer that night, he found himself telling Morris about the time travel experiments and the plan to fight real pirates. Once Morris had heard the details of

Coco's and Eric's secret plan he was both intrigued and thrilled, insisting that he be part of it and said he was prepared to give it his full financial backing. He made it clear from the start that he didn't want to do any fighting as he was a pacifist, he just wanted to escape, this time, paint and be part of the crew.

The next day, Eric awoke with his head splitting with pain. He had a terrible hangover but was excited as he now had a backer with all the money he needed for the project to go ahead. He remembered through the haze of the evening's drinking that Coco and himself had been invited up to Morris's house to talk about time travel and work out the logistics of building a ship.

Eric did his best to get up. Keeping the curtains drawn, he made his way along the small hallway to Coco's room. Coco was up and dressed and reading a new book on the building of clockwork toys given to him by Greg. Laid out on his small bench in his bedroom were tiny clockwork parts and detailed drawings.

'Morning!' Coco shouted, grinning at Eric's grimace.

'Shh, shh, Coco please, my head is splitting, I had a skin full last night.'

Coco laughed and raced across the room to slap his friend on the back. Eric went over and drew Coco's curtains tightly, making sure that not the tiniest ray of light got through into the room.

Coco made his way out through the bedroom door as Eric reclined on his bed, placing the pillow over his face. 'I'll make you some tea, that will pick you up,' he said cheerily.

Eric sat up on Coco's bed, holding his head between his hands, and said, 'no, wait, Coco, I need to tell you some good news. I met a really nice; useful chap yesterday called Morris. He'll be the answer to our prayers as he wants to fund everything.'

Coco smiled. 'Wow, sounds fantastic! How did you meet him?'

Eric looked up and looked at Coco through bloodshot eyes.

'I met him in the small art gallery on the sea front. His name's Morris, he's an artist, a good one and wealthy too and he wants to fund the whole thing, building a pirate ship, machinery, the works. He wants us to go up to his house first thing so you can meet him and we can make plans and set the wheels in motion.'

Coco was amazed. 'Wow Eric, this is unbelievable! Come on let's go!' he said triumphantly, trying to drag his friend off the bed.

Eric flopped over to one side on the bed, saying, 'let's have that tea first and maybe a spot of fried breakfast just to settle my stomach a bit. I still feel drunk, the walls feel like they're falling in on me.'

Coco laughed and shot down the stairs to make the tea, put the big pan on the stove and lighting the gas under it, then adding a huge dollop of lard to it.

A few minutes later the smell of the salty, sweet bacon drifted up the stairs, pulling Eric to his feet. It wasn't long before he was feeling more human again and the two of them set off up the hill to meet Morris.

Morris had written directions on the back of a bar napkin. However, the house was easy to find as it was the largest in Cornwall and sat impressively on the cliff top overlooking the town centre. As Eric and Coco got closer to it, they could see that it had been built using large stones that were highly decorated and carved to form the impressive facade of the house. There were huge gardens and a long driveway which led up the property. As it was situated at the very top of the hill, it commanded great views over the sea and along the cliffs as far as the eye could see.

Eric rang the bell and an elegant Indian gentleman dressed in white with a turban and highly ornate gold jewellery, opened the door and ushered them through. The pair followed the Indian gentleman in silence whilst looking about them at the colourful luxurious furnishings and carpets.

Large oil paintings hung in every possible space in the hallways, right up to the ceilings. They depicted battle scenes on land and sea. They walked past them in wonder while they were led towards an open plan room leading off a side hallway. It seemed to be Morris's study.

The Indian gentleman bowed as he entered the room and gestured for the boys to go in before leaving the room, walking backwards and bowing again.

Morris went over and welcomed them in a jolly manner. 'Eric, my dear friend, how's the head?' he beamed.

Eric smiled and held up his hand, rubbing the side of his head, indicating that it was not so great.

Morris, laughing, took Coco's hand and said, 'So you must be Coco. Eric's told me all about you; it's an honour to meet you, a very fine honour indeed!'

Coco shook Morris' hand and smiled back. 'Thank you.'

'Now, my young friend Eric,' said Morris in a jovial manner, 'what you need is the hair of the dog to fix that hangover, but first a smoke.'

He looked knowingly at Eric before going over to a heavily carved teak box on the side table and taking out three fat cigars.

He handed one each of them, holding his under his nose and sniffing the cigar, admiring the fragrant quality.

Coco put his in a pocket, he didn't smoke, but did not want to offend Morris on his first meeting; so instead, tapping his pocket said, 'I'll smoke it later, with a glass of whisky.'

Eric peeled off the fine decorative paper wrapped around the cigar and, picking up the cigar cutters, snipped the end off and then put it in his mouth, waiting for Morris to light it.

The two of them pulled in deep drags of their cigars and then together let out puffs of smoke that filled the room, adding another coat of nicotine to the already yellowing ceiling.

Morris slapped Eric on the back in hearty admiration and gestured for them to sit down in one of the many large chesterfield chairs that adorned the room.

'Down to business,' said Eric. 'We need a plan. We'll need the ship, of course, but more immediately we need a meeting place where we can recruit the crew and be able to observe them and make judgment on their characters.'

Morris looked thoughtful and said, 'When I was living in London, I used to visit a gentleman's club. It was a place where men could come and read the paper in peace with no women. There was also a smoking room.'

'That sounds good,' said Eric, pulling a long line of smoke from his cigar and blowing large smoke rings upwards in an uneven fashion.

'It sounds boring,' said Coco, 'and we're only going to attract old men that way!'

Eric said, 'he's right. We need some young blood, men with a bit of fight left in them.'

Morris thought for a bit, and then he said, 'let's call it a gentleman's club, but make it a cross over with a sports club.'

'Yes, yes,' said Coco, getting excited, 'and then we can have fencing lessons and boxing.'

'We will need a large building for that,' Morris said.

'I have one in mind.' said Eric. 'It's large old place on the sea front; it looks as if it's been empty for a while, but it's large enough to even have boxing ring in the basement.'

Morris poured everyone a glass of whisky, then made a toast. 'The gentleman's club.'

He took a long swig of his drink, set the glass down to re-fill it and said, 'So then we have the club, of course, I will hand the day to day running over to the pair of you. My heart lies in the building of a pirate ship, and I have just the fellow in mind for that task.'

Morris drained his glass again and, refilling it to the top, said, 'and you, Eric, you will need some assistance with building the time machine. I have plenty of money so feel free to employ some more help if you can. There's a young girl called Samantha who goes by the name of Sam, a bit of a tomboy who works in the clock repair shop. She might be worth investigating as a potential employee.'

Eric made a mental note of Sam's name and then said, 'our good friend Greg will be coming any day now. I've already sent word, and my equipment is en-route. Greg is a clockwork toy inventor; he will help, but we also need a large space to work on the machine, somewhere away from the public's gaze.'

'That's fine,' said Morris. 'You can bring it all here, this house is huge, and there's only me and a couple of staff here, plus there are extensive outbuildings in the grounds. You can take your pick.'

Coco got up to admire a painting over the fireplace. 'This is very good.'

Morris seemed pleased. 'That's one of mine,' he said proudly.

The rest of that day was spent making many plans and sending telegrams around the country to organize people and equipment. Morris had many useful contacts and commissioned a ship historian and designer, arranged a team of boat builders and rented a large dry dock to build the pirate ship in.

The men agreed amongst themselves that they would tell the people of Falmouth that it was an art reconstruction and that when it was finished, they would be taking it on a long voyage. Morris was already known around Falmouth for both his art and his extravagance, so they were sure that the locals would think this plausible.

After a day of talking and a lavish evening meal, Eric and Coco finished the last of the whisky and then set out to explore Morris's grounds and buildings, the Indian gentleman in tow with a flashlight and a heavy set of keys. After half an hour they came across a very large empty iron framed greenhouse which had a yellow stone brickwork base and decided that it would be the perfect place to build the machine in as it had a lot of natural light, together with gas heating and lighting system.

Over the course of the next few weeks, the building for the gentleman's club was purchased, and Greg arrived with Eric's and his own equipment.

Morris got involved with the ship building, and his enthusiasm for the project and money got things moving at an amazing rate.

Coco and Eric took on setting up the gentleman's club. Coco was still worried that the club might attract overweight 'well to do' men, who looked like they had a fight to get out of their chair let alone crew a pirate ship, so he painted images of swords and boxing on the front of the building as a deterrent.

Greg did not stop from the moment he arrived and soon had the equipment for building the time machine unpacked and set up in the large old greenhouse, under the close supervision of Eric who moved into the potting shed at the side of it so he could be near the machine to work on it if he had ideas.

Eric had given him good instructions, but Greg had many of his own ideas as he had worked on designing and inventing many clockwork toys over the years.

A couple of weeks later the pair realized that they would need some more help, so Greg went down to the clock repair shop to find and recruit Sam.

The plan was to get Greg to employ Sam and for Eric to teach her about the time machine and how it worked. Sam was working and living in the clock repair shop in Falmouth. She was an apprentice, having been taken on at thirteen. She was now sixteen years old.

The clock repair owner also made clocks to sell in the shop. He liked the elaborate designs Sam invented and believed that she was naturally gifted.

Sam was tall for a girl. She had short dark hair and very pale skin. She appeared to have no family or friends, even though she had lived her whole life in the area, she had not mixed well with other people and partially disliked the teenagers of Falmouth.

As Sam lived in the workshop, she often worked until late into the nights on her own ideas for intricate clock parts and small machines.

When Greg went into the clock repair shop to find Sam, he went in under the excuse of wanting to purchase some cogs and springs, and the shopkeeper was more than happy to show him around. As it happened, the small shop was surprisingly well stocked, and Greg purchased many things for the time machine. He could not see Sam at first, but when the shop repair man took him into the basement to collect some new parts, he saw her at a dimly lit bench, working on an unusual clock.

Greg attempted to strike up a conversation with her. 'Hello, what's that you're working on?'

Sam did not answer at first.

The repair man laughed and said, 'oh, this is just my apprentice working on something or other.'

The shopkeeper tried to distract Greg with some crystals that he had just acquired from Austria, but Greg said, 'can we go and see what the girl's working on? It looks jolly interesting.'

Reluctantly, the shopkeeper took him over to Sam's desk; mumbling under his breath that Sam was getting too big for her boots and paying her attention would not help.

Greg was impressed by Sam's work and offered to buy her apprenticeship from the clock repair man and to pay four times the price so that she could to come and help work for him. The clock repair man did not seem that bothered as Greg gave him a lot of money to over-compensate him and there were plenty of less difficult teenagers he could employ as an apprentice. Greg also made another large order of clockwork machinery as an added sweetener.

Sam was a little taken aback at first and slightly cross at being bartered for like she was a farmer's cow. But when she got up to Morris's house and met Eric, who explained the workings of the time machine, she could not have been happier and was fascinated by the whole idea of the ship and time travel.

Sam was told she was to serve under Eric, learning how to repair and fix and operate the machine. Morris came to meet her and said she was welcome to come and stay rent free in his house and take her pick of the rooms. Sam excitedly ran around the large house before settling on a large empty bedroom which overlooked the sea cliffs and had an adjoining bathroom. Sam had never had a bedroom and bathroom to herself and for the next two weeks, she refused to work on the time machine, instead spending her time redecorating and taking long hot baths while reading books. She also set up a work bench so she could continue her work of designing clock parts in private. Her room was her own, and no one was allowed in it. She befriended the Indian gentleman, who promised to keep a strict eye on it for her and she carried the door key on a chain around her neck.

Meanwhile, the revamping of the building that would house the gentleman's club to make it look modern and appealing to younger men was progressing nicely and nearly finished. There was much talk and excitement about the club in the Falmouth and the surrounding areas.

The building itself was old, and its design was unusual for Cornwall, being of timber construction, white walls and black beams. It was not an original Tudor building, but it had been built in the style. Although tall for a building, it exhumed a regal air that Morris felt was needed for a gentleman's club.

It was agreed between the men that the club would be free to join; you only had to be a man. However, you needed to be recommended by two existing members. The drinks were the same price as they were in the local tavern and food was to be well made and offered at also comparable rates. So as not to put off potential members of this club, by the term gentleman, in the title, a lot of emphasis for potential members was put on the boxing ring and training. There was a pool table and card tables, fencing classes were held in the top most part of the building and boxing in the basement.

The staff was chosen by Morris, and he handpicked their uniform, black suits and bowler hats. There were rules, but not as many as you would think. The main one and least popular was no women on the premises. Fighting was allowed, however if a fight ever broke out it was swiftly encouraged to take place in either the boxing ring below the bar or the dwelling room above.

Morris employed a doctor, Miss Evelyn Heap, who lived in the club and fast became a permanent fixture. She was Scottish and very knowledgeable but slightly stern lady. She had worked for many years in the military hospital in Aldershot, before returning to Cornwall to nurse her then elderly mother, who had recently passed. Evelyn was in her late 40's, was strikingly good looking and well presented. She prided herself on her appearance and always dressed in a formal Victorian manner, long bustled dresses, a rigid corset and structured hats. You got the impression from talking to her that there was nothing much she had not seen. However, she was not well travelled, and she loved to hear of Morris's memoirs of his exotic travels and strange animals and felt she would have loved to travel if she could have a chance to live her life again. She had Thursdays off and, having no family left to spend her free time with, she used this day to help out at the local surgery.

After only a short time of knowing her, Coco decided to entrust Evelyn with their secret and invite her to take part. Evelyn was a woman of science, there were few woman doctors in this period, and she liked to stay at the forefront of medical science. She had a broad mind which was open to the new possibilities the century brought. At first, she had difficulty believing in time travel, but after Eric's demonstration of the robot teleporting, she was intrigued, honoured and excited to be taking part.

It was under Evelyn's discreet observation that Coco and Eric began the process of careful elimination of the men by whittling them down to a possible few who could man the ship and fight. Evelyn soon became invaluable to the group as she was a good judge of character and she was forthright in her option as to whether she felt the club members were of sound mind and would make good candidates for pirates.

Coco and Eric regularly met up at Morris' house to share progress reports over rum and talk deep into the night, and it was through these talks that they got to know more of Morris' life, and he became a trusted friend to them both.

Morris' story was interesting; he was a rich artist who enjoyed much popularity from his skilfully painted landscapes and battle scenes. His work was on display in Greenwich in London as well as hanging in the homes of many rich people and even European royalty. Morris was always asked to do portraits of the fat rich aristocracy; however, he never did, choosing instead to paint war and famous naval battles. He felt angry at the art scene about the category he was plumped into and about the people he had to mix with to get the commissions that he wanted.

One old rich retired admiral, who was his greatest fan and who commissioned many of his paintings, had become one of his best friends. The admiral had told him of the many adventures and battles he had fought. When the Admiral died, he left everything to Morris, as he had no descendants to pass his wealth on to and no blood relatives that he liked. The Admiral's house was a cross between a castle and a fortress.

Although Morris had everything now he could want, he was bored, and he had travelled the world, but as a single man found it to be stifling. Plus he was gay. The Victorians had strict rules about gay men; he lived in fear of being discovered each time he took a lover.

Morris had a second home in London, and it was here that he found he could mix better with other men who had similar interests, but always in secret and at night or in covert operations. He could never be open or relaxed which he found both tiring and frustrating.

Now that he was getting older he did not meet as many young men as he had in his youth. His best memories were of a time when he was young at art school in France, living in the artists' quarters of Montmartre in France near to the cathedral and going each night to music halls, drinking absinthe, taking drugs and mixing with the many artists who lived there.

He stayed in Paris for many years. Many times he felt he should return to his home in Cornwall but each time a new young man would take his fancy, and he would put off leaving. It was when his art started to take off that he made the return trip to England. He had exhausted his savings and the years of merry making had taken their toll on his bank account. He was given three large commissions of Napoleon's battle by his future benefactor, who admired Morris's brush work and attention to detail. Having been in the Navy, his whole life was quite used to homosexuals and so was quite at ease with Morris. The pair struck up a lasting friendship.

When in London, Morris had fallen for perhaps the love of his life, although, at the time, he had not realised it. They stayed together for ten years, but alas his gentleman friend died of consumption. Morris faltered in his work, unable to stay in London as every place reminded him of his lost love. He went to Cornwall and moved in with a retired admiral where he painted and had a quite comfortable life. He never fell in love again.

Morris was a portly man and not at all physical. However, he was a keen sports fan and, in particular, he enjoyed watching a good fight.

The boxing ring had been installed in the gentleman's club, which proved popular with the younger lads of Falmouth. The boxing ring was in the large basement which had no windows, just gas lamps to light it, which reflected off the white brick walls. The fighting shadows under the glow gave strangeness to the walls and added to the overall excitement of the experience. The boxing coach, handpicked by Morris, trained the lads and gave the rules. Sometimes there were bare knuckle fights and betting took place on them. Coco learned to fight along with the boys and became good friends with one lad in particular called Jude.

Jude was about the same age as Coco. Jude was a short, plain looking boy. He was also plain speaking, being descended from farmers and that's what Coco liked best about him. Jude's parents wanted him to carry on farming. However, the family did not own the farm; they just worked it for a rich land holder who kept the farm running on a tight budget. There was not much excitement being a farmer and hardly any profit to be made for the family. It was hard work and long hours, out in all types of weather. Jude did not mind being outside; he just was fed up with the life and often dreamed of travelling and seeing the world.

Jude had a mass of think lank hair which he kept unfashionably long and sported a thin moustache, which he was proud of as not a lot of lads could grow one at his age.

Coco admired his moustache and Jude joked, 'well, we come from a hairy family. I'm sure we have woolly sheep somewhere in our ancestry.'

The pair laughed and joked a lot. As Coco had grown up just with Mary and no brothers, he started to begin to think of Jude a bit like his twin brother. The more time that they spent together the closer they became and after a year of friendship even finished each other's sentences.

Jude was curious about the strange growths on the back of Coco's neck, but he never asked about them. He just waited until the day that Coco would tell him under his own steam.

The loft part of the gentleman's club building was laid out with a bleached pine floor, white walls and large roof windows. Here was the place that the boys and the men practiced their swordsmanship. They weren't able to find anyone to teach them to fight using a cutlass. However, Morris employed a fencing master from France, who taught them not only the rudimentary skills of fencing but also such things as sparring, parrying, etc. Coco had received a letter that Mack was on his way to Cornwall, and he knew that he would soon introduce lessons with a bit more flair.

It was after a solitary practice fencing session between Jude and Coco that Coco decided to trust Jude with his secret.

'Jude, we've known each other a while now, and I trust you and think of you as my brother.'

Jude gave Coco an odd look and said, 'and I you.'

Coco looked Jude in the eyes. 'My friend, I need to tell you all about my life and how I got to this point as I would like you to be in my future.'

Jude nodded. He could tell this was going to be a serious conversation, so he put his fencing sword away and stood to look at Coco.

'Well, old man,' Coco said in a friendly manner that was soft and caring, 'I have a no knowledge about how I was born other than it must have been at sea as that's where I was found.

'I was looked after in my childhood by an old nun, Mary, who kept a journal of my young years. This journal is now my most prized possession.

'In it, Mary says that she found me one morning, washed up on a large seaweed bed. Mary made a note in the book to stay what a strange occurrence this was, not only of course to find a baby, but also for the large reed bed to have been washed up at all, as there had been no storm. The sea was completely calm. Mary had lived alone with her cats on the island for many years and had noted that she had never known such a reed bed like this to be washed up.

'In her words, it was as if it had been pushed there from out of the sea and, being very religious by nature, she decided that, it must have been God that had pushed the reeds and baby to her. She had given up her life to serve God and, having no family to speak of in her older age, she was used to miracles having witnessed them her whole life, so my arrival was a gift that she accepted.

'She was a caring old woman; she had been a nurse before she found God and given her life to him. In her younger years of service, she had been a missionary travelling across the world to parts of deepest Africa teaching the children and spreading God's love.

'But although she loved her life on the island and her many cats, there was still this secret belief she had kept hidden even from me, that she would have liked children. She wrote this near the end of her journal.

'So you see, she believed in her strange way that I was a gift from God to her.'

She also kept goats, so she fed me on goat's milk. She named me Pinocchio from one of her favourite stories; she loved to read and also read me many Bible stories as well.

'She shortened my name to Coco as Pinocchio was too cumbersome, which by luck fitted in well when I got to the circus.'

'The circus?' Jude said, his eyes widening.

'Yes, you see, my poor Mary lost the plot and threw herself off a cliff. The ownership of the island reverted to the church, and I was sent to live in an orphanage. It was a horrible place, and they were going to operate on me to remove the tubes from the back of my neck.'

Jude looked up at his friend and asked, 'I had been meaning to ask about them, um, what they are? Err, is it a family disorder? My family has a strange type of growth disorder and were a bit of an odd mix. I wondered if it was something like that.'

'Your family have a growth disorder? I have never heard of such a thing, are you ok?'

Jude laughed, 'yes, luckily I don't appear to be affected, but my sisters are, one has a deformed leg, and the other has one leg longer than the other, and they all are covered in horrid looking brown hairy spots that look a bit mole-like. Also, they get these large lumps sometimes, they're quite harmless; they just look horrid.'

Coco looked concerned and asked, 'But you're all right, Jude?

'Yes I'm fine like I say, the family disorder didn't affect me. So, are the tubes on the back of your neck something like that, a family disorder then?'

Coco looked serious. 'No, I don't think so although I can never really be sure as I don't know who my parents were.'

'So Mary was allowed to keep you then? Why weren't you put in an orphanage when you were a baby?'

'I think her friend, Ann, who visited our island every fortnight, tried to persuade her to do that, but Mary loved me, she was very caring and taught me all that she knew. I learned to fish and milk the goats. Mary and I looked after each other and the island and grew things to eat.'

Jude looked thoughtful. 'So is there anything in that journal she wrote about the growths on your neck and who she might think that your parents were?' he asked in disbelief, questioning the story.

'Nothing,' Coco said. 'However, Mary was well educated, there was a large library on the island, it was well stocked with old books on every subject. The church and buildings used to belong to the monks, at one point it was an island just for men. But the monks pulled out of it years back, as the weather can be quite bad there.

'Nuns have no money, you know they give up all world possessions to the church when they join,' Coco said to Jude. 'So she wanted to live on the island, and as luck would have it, or fate even, some dotty old relative had gone out to America and struck it rich with oil, so bought her the island as a present, as well as all the furniture and like many of the books the monks would sell. As it turned out, that was most of them. This rich relation also paid for food and supplies, goats and the two boats for fishing. It all worked out well until Mary died.'

Jude smiled and patted his friend on the back.

Coco continued, 'It may sound an odd childhood, but Mary and I were very happy. She used to fish to feed all the cats, which did not come with the island. Her friend Ann that visited liked to rescue them and brought them out to her for company.'

'So you have no idea about the tube growths then?' Jude asked again, slightly disappointed after waiting all this time, wondering what the tubes were.

'Well, I was just getting to that bit. Mary believed that she had found similar things described in one of the books on an octopus.'

'Octopus?' Jude laughed.

'Not as funny as you might think,' Coco said, shyly, as he was not expecting him to laugh.

'I'm sorry,' Jude, said quickly as he realized that he had upset and offended his friend. 'Carry on.'

Coco stood up, went over to the door and locked it, and then walked back to stand directly in front of Jude.'

Slowly he unwound the thick canvas sling that he always wore on his left hand, took off the damp towel wrapping and, much to Jude's shock, out flopped an octopus' arm.

Jude scrambled back a bit in the room, he was only a country boy, and he had never been to a circus, so was shocked.

'It's fine,' Coco said. 'Really.'

Jude walked over and ran his hand over the arm, it felt cold, and the suckers all moved independently, the skin felt slippery and clammy.

'So were you born with his arm, too? Not to be mean, my friend, but no wonder the nun wanted to keep you alone on the island,' Jude laughed.

'Strange as it seems, I may never have acquired an octopus arm at all if it hadn't been for a terrible accident with a circus knife-throwing act,' Coco said.

Jude, now over his initial shock, was fascinated with the octopus arm, 'So what can it do? Can you fight with that arm?'

'Better than you would think!' Coco beamed. 'The arm somehow thinks for itself. Grab some swords and I'll show you.'

Jude grabbed his sword; Coco took two.

'Right,' he said, 'I'll face this way and pretend I'm fighting a person in front of me, and you stand at the back of me and go to attack me.'

'Yay yer,' Jude shouted, lunging at Coco from behind. The pair began to fight, Coco's octopus arm swinging around the room, the blade narrowly missing Jude as he jumped clear. Jude, still a bit unsure, started to fight back; he swung his sword fast and charged towards Coco. The octopus arm grew slightly and fought him back, after three attempts Jude fell back and finally gave up.

'How is that possible? You were fighting me, and you weren't even looking at me,' Jude said, questioning it all.

Coco did his best to explain. 'I know it's strange, it's like there're a brain and senses in my arm. I can also taste through the suckers and smell as well.

'However, just keep this to yourself as I've spent enough time being a freak when I was in the circus, and I'm way too good looking to be laughed at.'

'That you are, Coco, you are a handsome chap; all the girls say so. In fact, let's stop with the fight practice for the day and go and get ourselves a drink and give the Falmouth girls a chance to look at you.'

'You know we won't get served as we're not eighteen,' Coco laughed.

'Who said anything about going to a pub? Let's go down to the jetty, there's an old sailor down there who brews his own cider from the local apples. Scrumpy, he calls it, and it's as strong as you can get.' Jude made a dash for the door.

'Hold up,' shouted Coco. 'Let me just wrap up this octopus arm of mine and put my woolly hat on. I don't want to be scaring the ladies off.'

Jude passed Coco the towel and helped him roll up the arm and wrap a sling around his shoulder.

They both laughed and headed out of the door down the street and off towards the jetty,

When they got to the old sailor's shed, the door was open. They peered in though the gloom of candle light to see that the old sailor was smoking something very strange in his pipe. It had a strong peppery, flowery smell. As they walked into his hut, the pipe smell swept up to meet the boys in an overpowering way. Coco looked about the gloomy hut; it was sparsely furnished with nets hanging from the ceiling and a collection of rods and fishing tattle stacked neatly in the corner.

Jude took off his cap and nodded at the old sailor politely.

The sailor looked up at them in a welcoming way and in slurred speech he asked what he could do to help two such fine looking young men this day.

'Is he drunk?' Coco whispered to Jude.

'No he smokes opium, it comes from poppies,' Jude whispered back.

Jude marched over and stood in direct line of the old sailor. 'We've come to buy couple of jugs of your finest Scrumpy cider if you please, sir.'

The sailor looked up at the boys. 'Has thee the coins?'

Jude smiled and handed him some coins.

'Help yourselves and bring back my jugs, but before you go, come and sit with me and have a shot of rum. It's a cold day, and I've a hankering for company,' the old sailor said.

The two boys sat down next to the sailor on old upturned crates with bits of old carpet as cushions.

Then the old sailor dropped his head back and laughed heartily as if he had suddenly remembered and old joke and then stood up and brought over three odd shot glasses with pictures of the suits of cards on them. He put them down on an old flat sea chest in the centre that he used for a table.

As he poured out the rum, he started to tell a story.

Jude had heard the sailor's stories before, and they had always started the same way: with a cold morning.

The old sailor drank his rum back in one gulp and said, 'It was cold that morning, very much like this one. We were out at sea; been out at sea about three weeks all told. That morning it was dead flat; still, very still. It's not natural to see the sea as calm as that.' He shook his head, looked about him and then stared Coco straight in the eye before continuing.

'I can tell you, it sent a chill though my bones, I looked out across the flat sea and could see that there was a mist forming, icy cold, I could sense there was something a-coming.'

Coco sipped the strong rum; his eyes fixed on the old sailor.

He took off his cap and turned to face them, then reached up, popped out his fake eye and put it on the makeshift table. Jude had seen this before; Coco hadn't and, in spite of living in the circus with all the freaks, was still a little shocked. He nearly spat out his mouthful of rum, but at the same time was also interested.

'Har har!' the sailor continued, delighted that he had their attention.

'This was the day I lost this,' he said, pointing to the now gaping hole in his face.

'So what happened?' Coco asked, holding his now empty glass up in the hope that the old sailor would refill it.

The sailor took a long drag from his opium filled pipe, the smoke snaking from the corner of his mouth, and then he reached over and filled all three glasses up to the top.

'Uh har,' he said. 'It was the mistress of the sea; the Kraken she had awakened.'

He pointed to an octopus-like sketch scratched into the paintwork on the wall. It showed a large octopus attacking a small ship and dragging it down below the waves.

'Yar! The fabled Kraken octopus monster, when it awakes it takes the ship in its loving arms and with its sharp beak it breaks it apart, and that's what happened, I swear it to you. She came across our bow and wrapped the ship in her deadly clasp. A splinter from the ship's wood gouged out my eye clean from its socket.

'I escaped by a whispered breath. By chance one of the small boats on the ship dropped off, and when we jumped in the water we managed to swim around and climb into it just as the ship sank, and we rowed away. The kraken was too busy devouring its prize, the large ship. So we was lucky, we sailed away, but alas without my eye. However, my friend the watchmaker here in Falmouth made me this new one and I look like my handsome self again.'

Coco picked up the artificial eye and looked at it; he could see it had tiny clockwork movements in the back. He held it up to his eye and was amazed that he could see through it like it was a telescope.

He placed it back on the table and said, 'So, how did you get home?' Coco had enjoyed the story but thought that there was a hole in it. 'I mean, you said you had sailed a long way, three weeks out at sea.'

'Well, luck, say I,' the old sailor said. 'We must have been drifting for a day; we was getting mighty thirsty and then out of nowhere the mist began to creep in again. I was worried that maybe she'd come back to finish us off. We started to sing to keep our spirits lifted. We sang a silly song that my ship mate used to sing as a child.' The old sailor coughed as if clearing his throat, picked up his cap and held it over his heart as if he was about to say a prayer and in a deep monotone voice sang;

"I'm grateful for the pineapple,

'I like the sweetness of the pear,

'Eating apples make me happy,

But prunes fill me with despair.'

Coco and Eric began to snigger, but the old sailor gave them a stern look with his one good eye and in a serious tone said,

'I shall tell you, boys, but you're not to repeat it, I was getting mighty scared, I thought my time was up. Then from out of the gloom we heard a fog horn. 'Moor our,' the old man said, flailing his arms apart, trying to make a noise like a fog horn.

'It was a haunting sound, it echoed though the mist, it was like an angel calling out to us. We all let out a cheer and then called out madly. It was an old tug boat, "The Penny" it was called, a jolly looking boat, white and red, the captain saw our boat and rescued us all.

'Once aboard he used some basic first aid to patch my eye up. But I was lucky; I didn't go down with the ship. Some of the hands did, you know.

'It was hard to come back to port and to face the families who lost men. It's a small place, Falmouth, and the fishermen families know each other.'

He sat silent for a moment as if lost in a faraway thought, then said, 'Sad times,' before pulling again on his pipe. Then his good eye glazed over and closed.

The boys picked up their jugs of cinder and sneaked out, laughing, and ran down to the sandy beach to drink. On the beach, there was a small wooden shed from which a plump lady with a face as red as a cooked lobster was selling homemade pasties. Coco bought them one each, to have with the cinder.

'Shouldn't drink on an empty stomach,' he said to Jude.

'Any excuse for a pasty!' Jude exclaimed.

After the pasty and cider, Jude had to go back to work on the farm, and Coco made his way happily back up the hill to Morris's house, staggering and hiccupping slightly.

Back at Eric's house, Eric was delighted to discover that Mack and Michelle had at last arrived with all their belongings. Eric agreed that he would give his parents' house over to them to live in as a couple as Coco, and he was now mostly living in Morris's house. Eric wanted to take them up to meet Morris right then but Michelle wanted to clean the cottage which had been left quite unloved with just the boys living in it. She told them that they should go up and get out her way so she could get on with the cleaning in peace, so Eric took Mack up to the house. Mack was really excited and already in pirate mode. He had a cutlass which he had built into his circus act so he could practice more. When they reached the house, Mack was impressed with its size and the elaborate style. The Indian gentleman let them in and told them that Coco and Morris were in the study, so Eric led the way and Mack studied and admired each of the paintings in the hall as he passed them.

Mack strode into the study, his full six-foot figure filling the door frame. He was an impressive figure of a man. Instantly Morris liked the cut of his jib.

Mack was dashingly good looking, soft black curls framing the soft burnt umber tone of his skin. His dark eyes gazed around the room and met Morris' in a welcome stare.

Morris was leaning back in his chair, but seeing Mack enter, he sprang to his feet and paced over to him, gasping his hand.

Coco had already filled in much of the details of how Mack was an ideal candidate for the crew; he had told Morris how Mack was an excellent swordsman and how he could speak Spanish and navigate by the stars.

'Welcome,' said Morris. 'Coco has told me all about you and that you're up for coming on the voyage back through time to fight real pirates with us.'

Mack smiled and took out his cutlass and waved it in the air. The light from the blade sent prisms of tiny rainbows which shone around the room, partially blinding Morris.

'Arrh!' Mack cried heroically, as he slapped Morris on his back in a friendly gesture.

'Good to have you here with us at last, my friend,' Coco said, taking out his blade and walking towards Mack. The pair exchanged pleasantries and admiration.

Morris went over to a small globe-shaped object and took a large dusty bottle of aged rum out, pulling the cork free with his teeth while Coco held three glasses bunched in his hands so Morris could fill them.

'A toast,' said Morris.

'To the voyage ahead!' Coco chorused.

'I will salute with you,' Mack said, grasping the glass and holding it high, 'but I will not drink with you, as I don't drink alcohol.'

'I respect you for that,' Coco said, clinking his glass against Mack's.

Morris drunk his rum down and, filling another glass, said, 'I take my hat off to you, Mack, as you are a far braver man than me to go up into a fight against deadly cutthroat pirates without a drop of Dutch courage in you.'

Mack watched as Coco downed his drink and said, 'wow, you have grown, Coco, in this last year, you're turning into a real man now. Have you been practicing your swordsmanship?'

Coco smiled and said, 'I have, and we have our own club now, but we're lacking a real sword instructor, we just have a fancy French one, so I'm hoping that you'll help train up our future crew, Mack.'

'Be glad to, Captain Coco,' Mack laughed.

Coco beamed with excitement and putting his empty glass down, said, 'Come on, I'll show you the club right now!' Mack smiled, and the pair said goodbye to Morris and Eric and walked down the hill towards the club with Coco chattering the entire way excitedly.

Coco, although he had the octopus growth on the back of his neck and his arm in a sling, was still very good looking. All the girls in Falmouth would stop to admire him and giggle as he passed. Normally he would stop and smile back, but he was oblivious to them that day, as all he could think about was that Mack was here, and now he could show him the club and how the adventure was nearing the start.

Mack was all too aware of the attention he got as the good-looking newcomer, but now he watched Coco stride down towards the club with such confidence like his head was in the clouds. Mack noticed all the female attention that Coco was also getting and smiled at his friend and gave him a wink.

'So, Coco, my friend, I see that you keep your octopus arm wrapped up in a sling and use your hair and woolly hat to hide the growths at the back of your neck,' Mack said, smiling at his young friend, and added, 'I can see that living in Falmouth is doing you good, you look well and happy.'

Coco smiled back and said, 'yes it is, Mack, all the preparations for the replica pirate ship and the crew and time travel are so exciting, I am so happy that we live in this time in history, with all the advancements and new machinery.'

The pair chatted to each other excitedly as they walked down the hill towards the club.

Mack was impressed with the club when he saw it. Coco ran in and almost knocked over Miss Evelyn in the hallway. She dropped the pile of paperwork she was carrying, and it shot it the air, having been caught by a breeze.

'Slow down!' she told him, half smiling.

Mack hurried past Coco and rushed to collect the papers. Coco apologized and jumped about, catching the last few.

It was Mack who handed Miss Evelyn the last piece of paper and stood for a second smiling at her, she looked up and seemed almost to be lost in his deep brown eyes for a moment. Blushing slightly, she whispered, 'thank you.' Coco grabbed Mack's hand and pulled him up the stairs. 'This is Mack, he's come to teach cutlass fighting. I'm taking him to see the fencing room.'

Miss Evelyn laughed at Coco's excitement.

Mack shouted back down the stairs, 'nice to meet you, your name?'

'Evelyn, Miss Evelyn, I'm the doctor so you will see more of me.'

'I hope so,' Mack smiled and then let Coco pull him the last few steps and out of her view.

Miss Evelyn felt slightly breathless she was not sure why, but she was sure it was something to do with Mack voice, it was as if he had taken her breath away for a second and she felt giddy like a teenager. Having a scientific mind, she decided that this was an irrational thought; she was far too old for these silly immature feelings. Still she took a hanky out and wiped her brow, took the paper work into her room and settled herself quietly in her favourite chair to sip sweet tea. There was something very magnetic about Mack and, try as she might, over the next few months she felt drawn to watch Mack practice his swords at every opportunity. Mack noticed her and always stopped to smile at her at every opportunity. He even blatantly showed off at times when she was around and would bring her wild flowers he found on the coastal path on the way to the club each morning, which became the highlight of her day.

Mack was a fine teacher, and it was not long before he had trained the boys in cutlass sword fighting and men who wanted to be pirates were knocked into shape.

Sam had been working with Greg and Eric on the machine; she was a naturally talented craft person and soon had learned all the intricate works of the machine including how to mill new bits if they broke. She was a hard worker but not that pleasant to be around as she did not like to waste time on a conversation or feminine things even although Michelle tried many times to get her to come clothes shopping with her or take afternoon tea.

Sam was a tomboy and liked to keep herself to herself and often could be found working as far away from the others as possible, long into the darkness of the night.

One day, however, Sam did speak at a meeting that Morris had called for them all in his house. Morris had arranged a lavish dinner, with guinea fowl, partridge and goose. He had hired extra help from the village to serve it and had arranged a local quartet to play for them during the meal.

Everyone chatted excitedly about their days, while being careful not to talk about the time machine in front of the people who were serving the food.

After the splendid meal, Morris invited them all into his study and offered the men cigars. To his surprise Sam got up and took one, she sat back in the chair and puffed out large clouds of smoke, coughing intermittently.

'Steady there, girly,' Morris said, pouring a large shot of rum and handing it her.

Michelle stared at Sam; she could not quite make her out. Sam looked back at her. 'What you staring at, Michelle? I work just as hard as Eric and Greg, even harder. I can do anything a man can do and better!'

'That's true,' chipped in Mack, 'perhaps that is apart from smoking a cigar.'

Sam threw the cigar into the fire, picked up a cutlass and flew at Mack as if to strike him.

Mack grabbed a poker and deflected the blow.

Sam raised her hand again to strike, dead centre, this time, aiming to bring the cutlass with one clear blow though his head.

Mack knocked the cutlass out of Sam's hand and pinned her tight to the wall.

'Steady on, guys,' Coco said, slightly alarmed.

Mack let go of his grasp of Sam, and she slumped down the wall then sprang up and flew at Mack, kicking him hard in the chins.

Mack keeled over with the sudden pain and stared laughing.

Sam was furious. 'Don't laugh, don't you laugh, I tell you!' Her face was red and puffy, her eyes blurred with anger and hatred.

'It's ok,' Eric said, in a calm manner to Sam.

Sam, still angry, went up to Coco and said, 'Captain, I want to learn to fight, I want to be a pirate like the rest of you. I have darn well earned it.'

Coco looked at the faces of the other men who seemed unhappy and shocked at the same time.

'A woman pirate, whoever heard of such a thing?' Mack sneered.

Morris chipped in. 'Actually there are records of women pirates and even a woman pirate captain.'

Coco said, 'well then it's agreed then, Mack, you can teach Sam.'

Mack stood up and brushed down his coat. 'Well,' he said, 'I would rather have her on my side than against me. We'll start tomorrow, Sam. Shake on it?' He held his large, strong hand out and Sam grabbed it and shook it hard.

As it turned out, Sam was as good at fighting as she was at machinery. She practiced with Mack every day, and Evelyn would always watch as the pair fought, in admiration of both Mack and Sam.

Evelyn had realised that she had fallen in love with Mack albeit from a distance, although she never said anything to him as she had met Michelle, his wife, a few times and knew of the deep love that Mack and Michelle shared. Also, she kept her feelings quiet as they would all be going on a voyage together and she had no intention of spoiling that. Evelyn had been in love once before, in her late twenties but sadly the man had been killed in an accident before they were married, so had accepted the role of a spinster. She had her work as a doctor, and that kept her busy.

Mack, with his kind heart, talent and good looks, was used to women falling in love with him and was fully aware of Evelyn's feelings. He tried his best to always pay her a small compliment each day as an act of kindness.

Evelyn began to live for those brief stolen moments when their eyes would lock, and she felt as if she had an electrical charge shoot though her body.

The next year passed quickly, and soon everything was ready for the main voyage.

So far this was turning into an interesting crew, Coco, Jude, Eric, Greg, Morris, Mack, Michelle, Sam and Evelyn. Six men and three women but there were many more men to join.

Chapter 6

(Arm 6).

Initiation Ceremony

All the chosen crew were gathered around a long table in the gentleman's club. Coco was seated at the head, but it was Morris who spoke first. He welcomed the men by offering his congratulations on being picked to take part in this epic voyage. He paused for dramatic effect and then announced that they were not planning to take the replica pirate ship on an art reconstruction voyage but aimed to go back through time and seek out and fight with real pirates.

Sam was stood next to Morris, the only girl in the room. She stared at the male faces, watching their reaction as they were told this news. She knew that she would be fighting alongside them if they chose to go.

The men seemed surprised and appeared to not sure what to say at first. Mumbling broke out between them. Jude said, 'is this a joke?'

Morris answered back firmly, 'no joke, it's deadly serious.'

The men gazed around at each other, not sure what to make of this sudden news. They had all believed the story that the ship was a replica and would go on a long voyage and had been excited about that. Now with this change of plan, everything was a quite new but also a bit unbelievable.

Coco stood up to address the men. 'I'm sure it's all seems unreal, and you'll have to make your own choice because we will be travelling into unknown territory, to another time and place. There will be many dangers, and we won't be returning to this period in history, so if you decide to come you will have to agree to it before we set off.'

Loud talking and many questions were shouted out from around the table but after just an hour of discussion, all who had been selected appeared to want to go.

A bottle of rum was passed around. Everyone poured a shot and held the glass in the air to make a toast.

Eric stood next to Coco and raised his glass high. 'Fellow friends, gentlemen and lady,' he nodded to Sam, 'it appears that we all have one thing in common, and that is to seek adventure and fight for real as pirates. Let's all drink to this and make a secret bond that will bind us to our ship, Captain Coco and each other.

Sam and the men cheered and clinked their glasses together before downing the rum.

Coco said, 'We will, in a few days, be sailing the high seas back in the distant past, when things of this modern time will be only the stuff of dreams to the young men we'll meet. However, we'll have a responsibility, to find adventure and strive to be the real heroes that we believe we are deep inside us. Charge your glasses again, pirates, and we shall have a toast to our voyage!'

Sam passed around a new bottle of rum, and they all chorused, 'to our voyage!'

Greg stood up and said, 'Without the constraints of modern society, we can be true to our hearts. Let us sit in silent for a moment and contemplate where we shall go in the future. When I say in the future, I mean in the past.'

Everyone sat in reverence, looking bleakly at each other across the room. It was hard to even begin to believe that soon they would wave goodbye to their lives in this time and be swept back to another time, a time where you could fight and even kill in a deadly battle with no rules and not be held accountable for your actions.

After a moment, Greg said, 'so, if anyone has any more questions or worries, now is the time to say them. Spit them out now, as there will be no going back. You'll have made your bed so will have to lay in it as we will not be returning again to this time frame.'

Jude slowly raised his hand. 'Sir, I am just a bit unsure, you know you said that we can kill pirates in the past, but what if we by chance kill one of our own ancestors, could we run the risk of ourselves being born?'

Some of the men laughed, but Eric said, 'no, this is a good question. However, Jude, think about it for a moment. We're going back in time, but we're travelling across the seas, there would only be a very slim chance that we would meet a direct ancestor.'

Greg chirped up. 'Yes that would be a rare thing; I mean you'd have to be pretty unlucky. However, if you think about it logically, then it must be ok.'

'How come?' Jude asked, curious.

'Well,' said Greg, 'we're all still here, so when we travelled back in time, we had already been born into this time.'

'But wait!' Jude said, confused trying to get his head around the whole idea of time travel, 'would we still be born? Will the time travel not cause an endless loop? I'm so confused.'

Greg sounded confident as he answered Jude, aware that the whole room was now staring at him. 'It's a strange concept, and I've dedicated a lot of thought to it and am of the understanding that it will be fine.'

Jude asked, 'how can you be sure that this time travel will work? I mean, have you done any tests and things?'

Eric spoke. 'Yes, I'm convinced everything will be fine. I've carried out many experiments and have made many small jumps back into time just to see if my instruments are correct and, as you can see, I'm fine, and I can tell you that nothing has changed.'

'Wow,' said Jude, and everyone whispered around the room.

Sam uncovered a model of the pirate ship, and there was a loud buzz of excitement. The men stood around it, she pointed to the clockwork parts and took the time to explain every detail of time travel as simply as she could and Eric and Greg answered every question.

Jude suddenly got quite excited. 'I can't believe it! At last, I can escape this humdrum existence in my life and live a life of adventure and danger, living life to the full, risking myself in the darkest parts of the sea.'

Then everyone started to get excited, and some scuffles broke out between the men, who were talking in pirate form and waving their swords around.

Eric banged his fist on the table. 'I'm calling this meeting to order.'

Coco shouted 'Order, order! Listen to Eric!' his voice bellowed around the room.

Eric waited for the noise to quieten down and then said, 'Ok, so in the last experiment I only set the dial to go back two days. Sam and Greg helped me; they monitored the equipment. Two days ago I went back and posted a letter just to myself so that I could check that I was jumping back in our timeline and not into some parallel universe.' Everyone looked blankly at Eric but were intrigued. Eric continued, 'then this morning, first post, there came my letter through the door. And here it is!' He held up his letter triumphantly.

Everyone cheered and banged their feet on the floor.

Eric waved his hands to silence the men. 'That was just one of many experiments. Sam and Greg have both travelled back in time for a week successfully, and I brought them back into this time again, unscathed.'

'It's true!' Sam said. 'There's nothing to fear.'

'Hurrah, hurrah!' The shouts and cries went up from the room full of enthusiastic men.

Eric beamed, 'Look at us! We already sound like a group of cutthroat pirates!'

Eric was so very happy; Coco was very happy. Just then the doors opened and in came Evelyn, pushing Michelle in a wheelchair.

Mack rushed over and greeted Evelyn with a warm smile and then went down on one knee and kissed his wife on the cheek and said, 'my fellow pirates, it's time for you to know my wife's secret. She's not an invalid confined to this chair; she is, in fact, a mermaid who came ashore to live with me.' He said this with his face beaming with pride and his heart full of such love it felt it was bursting.'

Michele pulled the blanket off which had been covering her chair, revealing her beautiful, stunning rainbow and silver coloured tail.

All the men gasped then cheered.

After they all had quieted down, Jude asked, 'What happens now?'

Morris stood up and said in a serious tone, 'Well, the launch is in two days, so say your goodbyes, make your peace and settle your affairs. Tomorrow morning 8 AM sharp be on the ship for a briefing.'

After several more hours of drinking, they went home.

The next day all the new crew members came down to the ship. They sailed away from the harbour and Eric manoeuvred the ship into a cove. Coco ordered that all the crew lined up in a row on the deck. Coco stood in front of them. He was like an army general giving a talk to his troops. He was already dressed in his pirate clothes.

He looked dashing; he was very good looking, tall and thin with a long neck, pale skin and bright eyes. His long curly hair was tied back and he was sporting a pirate's hat which had a white plume in it. He had black knee length boots which had large brass buckles on the front. His large cutlass was in its scabbard, attached to a sling-like belt hooked over his shoulder.

You could see the octopus's tubes like growths at the back of his neck, but they did not distract from the fact that here, stood in front of his crew, he looked every inch a pirate.

Eric admired Coco's clothes. 'No wonder the girls go weak at the knees over you, 'he said to his friend, slapping him on the back in a manly way.

Coco smiled, he had caught a look at himself after he had finished getting dressed and even he had to admit he looked good and, more importantly, he looked the part.

Morris had arranged that all the crew had pirate clothes; there was no set uniform or even colour to wear. Coco had always liked the colours green and blue, so his clothes reflected that. Mack chose grey, Eric and Jude blue, Sam green and Morris rose pink.

It was a still, damp morning. Eric anchored the ship and set up a cloaking device, so it could not be seen. However, at this time there was not much chance of that, it was just in case the fishermen were out, pulling up the lobster pots dotted around the shoreline.

Coco cleared his throat and addressed his crew. 'Men, I am sure all of you have noticed the growths on the back on my neck.' They all mumbled and looked at the floor, but no one said yes.

Coco continued, 'Well, the growths are something I appear to have to be born with or at least acquired when I was at a very young age. I know that the growths look quite ugly, which is why I make efforts to cover them if I am out in public. However, they have a use. I discovered that if I want to swim backwards fast underwater, somehow I am able to breathe through them and propel myself backwards at great speed.

'So that is just one of the things that is unusual to me. The other is this!'

Coco unstrapped his octopus hand, and it slapped down on the deck, making a noise a bit like a wet fish being landed.

Some of the crew looked shocked. Coco extended his arm out to his full length; it must have been over-six-foot-long, and the suckers moved about expectantly. 'These suckers,' Coco said, 'can taste, feel and also do things independently; it's like some of my brain has developed into this arm.' He waved it above his head.'

Eric cheered, and all the crew joined in.

Coco lifted up a sword with his octopus hand and waved it at Eric. Eric took out his sword and waved it back at Coco, and the pair had a mock battle which Coco won.

'So, fighting well with this arm is one of the talents I have. Also, I can squash into small places and camouflage myself into my surroundings.

'However, the best thing of all, I will show you as part of this pirate initiation ceremony.'

Eric stood in front and bowed down in front of Coco. Coco wrapped his octopus arm over Eric's neck and then in one moment he used one of his suckers and sucked on the back of his neck.

This left a mark in the shape of a whelk; it was over quickly and did not hurt.

Eric got up and walked around; he wanted all the crew to see the mark and not be scared.

'Men, I need you to trust me, there is a reason for this,' said Coco, raising his voice above all the mumbling.

Jude came forward next and knelt down in front of Coco and Coco moved his arm over Jude's neck and then did the same to him, leaving a whelk shaped mark on the back of his neck, like Eric's.

'It doesn't hurt,' Jude said.

Mack went next, then Sam and Morris and then all the remaining crew lined up to receive their whelk marks, then they lined up again.

'Now, crew,' said Coco in a strong and clear voice, 'please do not be alarmed at the demonstration I'm about to give. But first I should tell you how I discovered this about myself.

'When I was nine, I discovered that when I needed to, I could pump the blood around my body fast and become really strong. This happened by accident as an octopus had ended up on shore, and some children were bullying it. So, even although I was much younger and smaller than the children, I was able to become somehow superhuman and rescued it by lifting it up and throwing it into the sea. As I lifted the octopus, its suckers touched me and somehow changed me, as from that moment on I could sense and hear octopus.

'I have thought about that incident, although at the time I was not sure of the full significance of that day's events. It was a long time after, when Eric and I first came to live in Cornwall I was out walking alone along the beach one early morning and felt like going for a swim. There was no one about, so I slipped out of my clothes and undid my octopus arm from its sling.

'I swam on by back, using the tubes in my neck like I had already described to you.

'When I was about five miles out, I floated, resting on my back. Into my mind came the vision of that octopus I had rescued that day when I was a child. I felt sad; it was almost as if I was singing a silent song in my head. And I felt my octopus arm tingle.

'Then from below me, I felt a movement in the water. Surging up from underneath me came a group of large octopuses. Their feelers felt me all over my body. I lay still and floated on my back in the water, just relaxing and breathing deeply though my nose and mouth. Then I felt complete peace, I felt overwhelming happy, like I had been on a long trip far away and had come home.

'I felt the love that Mary, the nun who brought me up and also the love of my own mother, who I knew, at that instant, had died at sea. I felt as if I was in her womb and could hear her heart beating.

'I understood that each child knows the unique rhythm of their mother's heart and that this sound stays as a trace memory until death becomes a welcoming comfort in the end. I understood that somehow I was deeply connected to the octopus as I could at that point hear their hearts beating and understand their unique rhythms.'

All the crew looked at Coco. His face was shining like it had tiny lights all over it.

Coco walked forward to the edge of the boat and thrust his octopus arm into the sea. 'I discovered that day I am part octopus, and I can communicate with these intelligent and beautiful animals.'

Coco turned to face his crew and, in a sober tone, issued a warning, 'Now, crew! I don't want you to be scared about what happens next. I must tell you that you must remain really quiet, no shouting or moving.'

As Coco's arm reached the water's surface, the there was a movement from below the ship. It rocked slowly from side to side. Some of the crew looked a little worried, but all held their spot and stood firm.

Jude was rooted to the deck just opposite Coco, and it was his face and his reaction that he studied as three large octopuses began to slide on deck.

He could see the shock on Jude's face. 'Stand firm, men,' Coco insisted.

They all stood still as three octopuses slid over the decking with ease. The octopuses inspected each of the crew with their tentacles and then, once finding the whelk mark, let go of them and moved on to the next.

It was not long before all of the crew had been inspected by the octopuses. Coco slumped to the floor and pulled his octopus arm out of the water, and the octopuses returned to the depths of the sea.

'What just happened?' Jude asked, stunned by the event.

'It's hard to explain it fully,' said Coco. 'As I've said, I can communicate with the octopus, I told them, you leave those who have a whelk mark. When we go back into time and fight the pirates, if that ship starts to fire on us, I will use the octopuses to destroy their cannon.

'I won't call them to fight for us unless we are in real peril.

'It's just we will have the one ship and will be miles out at sea, so can't risk that it will get damaged. So if we disable the cannon on our opponent's ship first, then it will be down to just hands on fighting and boys, that's what we are after, that's the whole reason for use going back, to fight and have adventures.'

'And no rules either!' Eric chipped in.

'Greer Yar,' shouted the crew, waving their cutlasses in the air.

'I have one rule,' Coco said, 'loyalty to all you crew, that's a given. However, I don't want anyone to kill a man who is unarmed, or has surrendered. No knifing anyone in the back!'

Everyone nodded in arrangement and another cheer went up.

Jude said, 'so our cannon, the ones shaped like octopus, they are just for show then, they don't fire?'

'Well, they can fire. However, I am hoping we won't need to use them; we are not going to go back to simply blow the other ships clear out the water. Where's the fun in that? No, we need to fight, so we don't fire the cannons off randomly.' Coco looked serious. 'So, time to swear an oath then, boys!'

Morris came out; he had a parchment paper document and a white feathered quill pen. 'You each sign here,' he said holding it up for them to see. 'And know this; there will be no going back once you sign!'

⁂

Coco's adventures continue in Book II, Time and Tide, coming soon!

⁂

About the author:

Jane Yates is a dyslexic mother, artist, and storyteller. She lives in Oxford, UK.

She is a steampunk young adult author who writes about time travel and sci-fi.

Octopus Pirate is her fifth book. All the books are easy to read and translate, ideal for people who are studying English.